EVERYTHING TO
LIVE FOR

BY PAUL HORGAN

NOVELS

The Fault of Angels
No Quarter Given
Main Line West
A Lamp on the Plains
A Distant Trumpet

Far From Cibola
The Habit of Empire
The Common Heart
Give Me Possession
Memories of the Future

Mountain Standard Time (*containing* MAIN LINE WEST, FAR FROM CIBOLA, *and* THE COMMON HEART)

Everything to Live For

OTHER FICTION

The Return of the Weed
Figures in a Landscape
The Devil in the Desert
One Red Rose For Christmas

The Saintmaker's Christmas Eve
Humble Powers
Toby and the Nighttime (*juvenile*)
Things As They Are

The Peach Stone: *Stories from Four Decades*

HISTORY AND BELLES-LETTRES

Men of Arms (*juvenile*)
From the Royal City
New Mexico's Own Chronicle (*with Maurice Garland Fulton*)
Great River: The Rio Grande in North American History
The Centuries of Santa Fe
Rome Eternal
Citizen of New Salem
Conquistadors in North American History
Peter Hurd: *A Portrait Sketch from Life*
Songs After Lincoln

EVERYTHING
TO LIVE FOR

by Paul Horgan

FARRAR, STRAUS AND GIROUX ❧ NEW YORK

to
Ernst Bacon

But I have lived, and have not lived in vain:
My mind may lose its force, my blood its fire,
And my frame perish even in conquering pain;
But there is that within me which shall tire
Torture and Time, and breathe when I expire;
Something unearthly, which they deem not of,
Like the remembered tone of a mute lyre,
Shall on their softened spirits sink, and move
In hearts all rocky now the late remorse of love.

Childe Harold's Pilgrimage, cxxxvii

AT THAT TIME OF LIFE and for a little while in that summer of 1921, my cousin Max was everything I wished I were. When they said I must visit his family I was polite about it, not wanting particularly to go. But they all said he was handsome, so original, as they put it, and would one day be so preposterously rich, with all the girls drawn to him, and with every boy, even younger than I, sure to learn much from a few days in his atmosphere, that I saw I must agree to go, if only to please my parents.

My invitation to a house party for the Fourth of July came from my mother's first cousin, who was married to the senior member of the Chittenden family, a ranking partner in the great fortune known by their name. Maximilian was the only son of that branch. As such he was the principal heir of the five generations of manufacturing money which reached back to the time of the Revolution, when the family wealth began to gather in all its self-reproductive weight as a result of Chittenden-built ships needed by General Washington and the Colonies.

"Their place is so beautiful—so immense," I was told. "There will be parties, and swimming and dances, and the famous fireworks concert, and imagine that great stable of motorcars of every kind. Cousin Alexander even has one of the great private libraries in the country, and you can browse there if all the rest doesn't interest you."

"Does Max read?" I asked.

"How do I know? But he goes to Harvard."

"If they live in the country, how can they have enough people for dances? Girls, I mean?"

"It is the kind of country where every hill has a great house filled with relatives and friends and they all know each other. They ride together—everyone keeps horses, and they play tennis and polo *at home,* and swim. Why don't you want to go?"

"They'll all be so full of themselves and they don't know me at all."

"If it is your hay fever you're worried about, don't worry. The summer nights in Eastern Pennsylvania are cool, especially in the Chittenden Hills, and our nights are so warm here, you'll be happy to be away. And you love to travel. Yes, to go visiting people so rich is like traveling in a foreign country. And everyone says Maximilian is so charming—so like his mother. She was the bright star of our generation. —You'll go?"

"I suppose so," I said.

"Oh, darling Richard, who can pull a longer face over something nice!" exclaimed my mother, and my father said,

"I believe it is considered proper never to be impressed, when you are seventeen?"

They both looked at me with fond appraisal, and I saw that they were working to keep heart at the spectacle of anyone young as he came to the threshold of any test—especially one for whom they held every hope. Life, they knew and as I did not yet know, was a series of barriers to meet and cross until the very last and most mysterious one of all. They had fondly brought me to pass so many already, some small, some great.

"But I still hate summer," I said, needing to lose my position with at least one small personal flourish.

"Hate summer! When everybody else can't wait for it!"

I had recently learned to make a mysterious smile and I used it now, with fine effect.

❀ ❀ ❀

It was true that for many years summer gave me a vague, hollowed feeling of dread such as I knew in no other season of the year. For a long time I didn't really know this, but as I grew older, I began to recognize how summer in its rankness of growth was like my own body as it reached new dimensions and pricked me with new sensations, mysterious, inviting, but also bewildering. I had something in my mind akin to the sudden rains of summer—showers of thought that came as from behind hills which obscured their origin; and like summer rains such storms brought heat instead of coolness, and grasses seemed to swarm and tendrils to climb and cling within my desires as powerfully as they did in the woods and fields. Certain wild flowers had such power that they made my breath close in my breast when hot damp nights persisted. Summer demanded my distrust, for how could you be sure which leaf would or would not poison you, or thorn produce swellings which sent their allergens through the blood and caused running tears and blurred sight? What were equally disheartening about summer were its beauties, so that I thought of misery and delight as inseparable; and I always went out when we were in the country and walked or rode a pony in the meadows where blue air seemed to part for me as I went, and far away amongst hills the blue was so dense that I knew just the pan of water color which would copy it. My heart sank at the impossibility of saving on paper what I loved across the fields. Passing through the wild flowers and whiplike grasses which opened before and closed after me, I was accompanied by a garment of color and sound, a little flying tapestry of insects—bees, gnats, dragonflies, heavy wasps—with whom I seemed to have a mysterious pact of immunity so long as I paid them no attention. Even if the pony stumbled and I had to make a sudden motion of recovery they let me alone, only intensifying their singing drone as they flew in new space to keep their adjustment to my sweating bulk. On the days when hazes hung over the meadows, and nothing seemed to breathe or move, my suspended feeling of expectation and dread grew heavier. I learned what it meant when the barometer fell; and I wondered if my heart fell within me accordingly. What was going to happen? I had the sense that something was coming. If only I knew what, I could be ready, and summer would lose its steamy, enfolding menace. But nothing told me, and so I went around with a false air of confidence, and in shame rehearsed *how to be* in front of the long mirror inside my bedroom door. I never liked what I saw there, and I think now that if I were to make an account of my unseen life as it was in that summer long ago I would entitle it "Apology for My Body." Once overhearing people talking about me with my parents I heard the phrase, "the awkward age," and I grew hot with anger, not because it said so much but so little. "Awkward" came nowhere near describing my outer state and its inmost desperations, the most powerful of which was a desire to be somebody—anybody—else. But how to escape? We are prisoners of our very selves, and the prison could be seen, touched, caressed, pleased, wounded, in its substantial being, while always abided the conviction that the outlook for deliverance was hopeless. But if you would believe what you heard, perhaps love would deliver me? But I fell in love with somebody different every day, and nobody ever knew it. It was an exhausting profusion of passions, and I concluded that nobody else in the world, behind all their smiling or preoccupied or sorrowing faces, knew as much as I did about what life was actually like; for if they did know, how could they present their unalarming aspects to the world?

"Richard is such an even-tempered fellow," I heard. "So clean, always, so well-groomed, it must be wonderful to be so nice-looking and be so contented. So many young people throw themselves about so. . . ."

Yes, nobody knew anything, and all you could do was be what they expected and hope for escape into the cool of autumn, and the cold of winter, when you could always take comfort in the suppression of summer, when all acts of life seemed exaggerated, too close, too powerful; for how could you escape heat that lay over the whole world and made everything swell and climb and burst, in blind fulfillment of appointed nature? In winter, at least, it was possible to come in from the snow and approach the fire and control the light and make the world for yourself.

✳ ✳ ✳

Late in the morning of July 3rd Max came to meet me himself as my train made its brief stop between Philadelphia and Baltimore. They had telegraphed that I would be met, but I did not expect him. I had never seen him but I knew him at once. He was strolling amiably along looking with frank and charming curiosity at everyone, as though to ask their needs, which he would take steps to fulfill. The day was hot, moist and bright, the station platform and the stairs down to the pavement shone with grime, and everyone else looked weary and useless. It was impossible not to identify him. He was like someone moving in his own light.

"That's my cousin Richard!" he exclaimed as I approached, wondering how to risk addressing him.

"Yes."

"Let me have your bag."

Not awaiting, not expecting, an answer, he took it from me and in his hand it looked shabbier than ever, and my ship and hotel labels from Europe a summer ago seemed like schoolboy souvenirs.

"You have saved my life," he said, taking me down to the street where his car—an Isotta-Fraschini with its top strapped back, its long hood shining in fire-engine red, and its engine negligently running since it was a nuisance to start it each time by turning a key—stood exactly in front of a sign which read *No Parking.*

"How?" I asked.

"Nobody else is coming, they've all regretted at the last minute, and it wouldn't be a party with just us at Newstead. You make it one."

[6]

It was a responsibility, and he laughed at my expression.

"Jump in. —But don't be alarmed. My girl Marietta who lives here will be with us a lot, and we'll find things to do."

Things to do usually sounded ominous to me, but Max made the prospect seem unchallenging and bright.

We drove off through the city and into the rolling countryside at high speed made elegant by the way he drove and the rich drone of the car. In populated areas I thought various strangers recognized him, but he took no notice. He conveyed me with the air of one who often did kind and simple things for others, even though, as the wage earners on the sidewalks might say, "he didn't have to."

"What is Newstead?" I asked.

"My father's place. My grandfather built it. He was a collector. He was gone on Lord Byron. If you like that sort of thing you can see the manuscripts and editions in the library. He named the house after Byron's."

"Yes, I wondered. I remember pictures of it."

"Ours isn't a copy, just a sentiment. It is hideous, as you will see, and huge, I suppose. In a couple of minutes you can see it on top of the hill. I'm never going to live there."

He meant when he inherited his great share of the Chittenden resources, including his father's house.

"Who is Marietta?"

"I told you. She is my *friend*. Marietta Osborne. She lives on the *next* hill. She is coming with us tonight and we three are going out dancing. She will like you. I can tell that now. And if she likes you, you will like her. It is always that way with Marietta. If it is the other way, there is no hope ever. I am the only one she likes whom she began by not liking, but then we were children, and I always knew it would change,

[7]

and it has. I think her name made you smile. Does it sound too much *débutante* to you?"

"No, it didn't. I like it."

"Then you just smile a lot, is that it?"

"I don't know. I didn't know it."

"Well, anyway, let's make it a good house party, no matter what. My Ma can't wait to meet you. She says your mother was always the bright star of their generation."

I laughed at him for his light spirits and said,

"No, that's what my mother told me about yours."

"Women. They probably hate each other and go around being sweet to cover it up. —Look, there's the house. From here, it always looks like a state hospital, don't you think?"

He turned the car into a narrow country road which ran up and down over hills. Off to our left was a high hill, put farther by the blue haze of the day. On its crest was a heat-grayed fieldstone house. It had many wide chimneys rising from a great central temple which threw out long wings leading to lesser temples at each end. There was an impression of white columns and three browlike pediments at middle and ends. Woods broke up against the crest of the hill like great waves, leaving the top clear, except for formal planting.

"They've put you in rooms near mine, so we can at least talk without shouting," said Max.

At this he turned sideways to look at me. His eyes were swimming with fun in their shining gray light. He was dusky with tan over high color. His hair was bleached on top from the sun, but at the sides was a glossy light brown. He had a classic short nose and carved lips and a strong round chin. His profile belonged on a Roman medallion. You would have to say, implying no softness, that he had

[8]

extraordinary beauty, both of face and body, and that the flickering humor which played all through his very use of his features and gestures mocked his appearance and his state of being. He was three years older than I and in all that he indicated between us he elevated me to his own age. It was a princely grace for a senior at Harvard to bestow upon a second cousin in his last year of school.

※ ※ ※

Max devoted all of that first day to me. We made a fine spiral up the hill to the garages—it was necessary to use the plural—between the house and the stables. Max climbed out over the side of the car rather than open the door as I did and we walked away toward the semicircular conservatory at the rear of the house which overlooked the back entrance.

"Max," I said, "shouldn't the motor be turned off?"

"They'll do it," he said, opening the conservatory door for me. We entered into an indoor summer, where tropical plants hung in a sweaty stillness of regulated temperature. "This is Ma's department"—indicating the hot-house—"but it needn't bother us except that she loves to talk about it."

"Will I see her?"

"Not today, they say. She is resting." He did not say why. "And Pa is in town for something directorial. We'll lunch alone and then I'll show you around."

"I would like to see the library."

"Somehow, I thought so. Do you want a swim before lunch?"

[9]

"Do you?"

"Not particularly."

How like him, to propose or offer, and then show indifference.

"I think not, thanks."

Hoisting my bag to his shoulder with comic ease, he led me upstairs and far down a white paneled corridor to rooms at the far end of the wing. The door was open. He preceded me within and put the bag on a rack and said,

"Here you are. I'm just across the hall. If you want to wash up now, I'll meet you in my sitting room for a cocktail. It's great you're here. You'll have to tell me everything about yourself."

He left me in my high, large, square rooms—a sitting room with a fireplace and bookcases, a bedroom, and a bath with a huge marble tub long enough for the "petrified giant" I had seen in a traveling carnival sideshow years ago. It seemed insufficient merely to wash my hands in such surroundings, but in effect I had been commanded to do so, and I did, wondering why the grand scale and rich materials of such a house had an odor unlike that of any house I knew. There seemed also to be a special stillness about the place. Was it because Maximilian's mother—Cousin Alicia, or Lissy, as she was always spoken of—was resting? But surely where she rested was far enough away and sufficiently insulated by doors and fabrics to protect her. I suddenly realized how expensive it was to obtain perfect quiet.

I returned to my sitting room and tried out all the armchairs, and then looked out my windows. I could see a meadow below the rolling hill, where a paddock was prettily marked off by white rail fences to make an outdoor riding hall. The striped goal posts of a polo field showed beyond. A white dairy barn, with a dark roof like the lid of a chest, and fancy lightning rods, stood at the end of another meadow, where black and white cows grazed and seemed never to move. Where the hills rose opposite again, I saw a long rambling white house dappled with trees on the next hilltop, and I said, "Marietta Osborne." Between the two windows of the sitting room a French desk stood at right angles to the wall. A trim small armchair enclosed in varnished caning stood waiting before it. I sat down in it and reached for writing paper which bore the name, mail and telegraph addresses, telephone number, and rail junction of the house, with appropriate symbols, and began a letter.

"Dear Mother, Dear Father, I have just arrived and all is big, beautiful, and silent as the tomb. I am as it turns out the only guest. Max met me at the train himself, I thought they'd send a chauffeur. He is like a crown prince and I think he—"

Just then without a knock the door opened and he came in.

"What's keeping you? —Oh: writing letters."

Smiling splendidly he walked over to me and picked up my letter and read it as if he were expected to approve it before it could be sent. His air was so friendly and wholesome that a flicker of resentment died down in my breast. What in anyone else would have been an intrusion upon privacy seemed with him to be consuming interest, aroused by affection. He laughed and put my letter down and said,

"Yes, isn't it dreadful, all of it, most of all the crown prince business. I have been accused of it before. What were you going to say about me in the letter just as I walked in?"

I was going to write, "I think he likes me," but all I said to Max was, "I've forgotten."

[11]

"Well, you'll tell me later, in some way or other. Cocktail?"

I had never had one, only a little wine on occasions of ceremony at home.

I followed him across the hall to his study, as he called it. It was the same size and shape as my sitting room, but where mine was neat and arid in its luxury, his looked like a junkshop in which everything was particularly valuable. There were only two chairs free of litter. Window seats, sofas, chairs, the corners, the tops of bookcases, were cluttered beyond confusion—all merged into a thick random texture of books, papers, sporting equipment, sweaters, riding boots, a piece or two of bronze sculpture, beer mugs, and whatever. His desk supported a typewriter and four or five drinking glasses and bottles and a pile of papers of all sizes and conditions. It would have been more worldly if I had ignored the clutter, but he saw my astonishment, and he said with a laugh,

"Don't mind it. This is the one place I have told them they may not touch. I know where everything is, and feel at home here, like an old dog with a blanket nest full of ratholes. Every time I go away to college they try to straighten it up, but it doesn't take long for it to be made comfortable again. —I'll admit it isn't much like the rest of the house. I hope you don't mind."

Mind! I thought it distinguished beyond words to live in a mess, if that's what you wanted to do in the midst of riches.

"Of course not."

"Are you neat?"

"I suppose so."

"It doesn't matter if it doesn't bother you. —You know

something? Almost all my clothes are things I have bought secondhand. Really."

I looked at him, so splendid in his country tweeds and checks. He was stirring a drink at the desk.

"Yes," he said, "all these, and it doesn't mean I want anything that wouldn't do. I just like the old feel of somebody else's things."

Out of my self-knowledge, I said,

"Maybe you want to feel like somebody else, too."

"Richie, good shot!" he exclaimed with great high spirits. "I've wondered about that. I really don't know. My parents can't understand it. My Ma sometimes looks at me as if I had fleas. —Here's your drink."

We tipped our glasses to each other and had a drink. It was strong and bitter.

"Was that Marietta Osborne's house I saw through my window?" I asked.

"Yes. She rides over almost every day. We're going to pick her up tonight at seven-thirty. Do you like to dance?"

"I went to dancing school."

"That's no answer, though perhaps it is. But when you dance with her, it isn't really dancing. It is an ambulant conversation. If I try to get her to pay attention to the dance band, she puts her lips together and shoots her breath out through her nose and shakes her head and tells me I am impossible, who ever went to a dance in order to *dance!,* she means. Her father's a physician, besides being on our board of directors. —Do you manage with girls?"

His question muted me by its suddenness. He added,

"No, I mean, plenty of men in my class at college are still all confused about it, and usually all wrong. I just meant—"

He blinked both eyes at me like a kindly elder, and to close the subject comfortably for me, while giving me the benefit of every doubt, he said,

"The only way to manage is to take them for granted. Let's go down for lunch. We'll have it on trays in the library, since we're alone, and you like libraries. I believe they're ready for us."

With a rough slap on my shoulder blade he turned me to the door in his easy sense of command and trust.

🐝 🐝 🐝

A great hall or gallery ran the whole length of the central unit of the house. The illusion of beds of flowers was created by banks of potted plants set in bays paved with loose chips of white marble along the pale rose marble walls. Hitherto I had seen houses like this only in luxurious early movies and there all the grandeur was painted on canvas with occasional wrinkles in it.

We went along and then entered a great room which took all the first floor of the far wing. It was the library. Shelves, spaced between unstained walnut paneling where portraits hung, extended behind gilded grilles to the coffered ceiling. Two fireplaces faced each other at opposite ends of the room. Now in summer both were filled with tubs of flowering plants. A pair of immensely long refectory tables stood in the center of the room. They supported lamps, Renaissance bronzes, and folio volumes. Long deep velvet sofas were backed up to the tables. We walked to a corner of the room lighted by a standing lamp. Two easy chairs with low tables in front of them stood in a circle of light. We heard a small noise across the room in the opposite corner and Max called out,

"Oh, Andy, excuse us, we just came in to have lunch on a tray."

"Yes, of course," said Andy, coming up from his desk as though discharged by concussion. "I was just going out for mine. Excuse me."

"Thank you," said Max, and as the small young man left rapidly, we watched after him. He walked in a rocking gait somehow appropriate to his general appearance, which, with his pale fuzz-clipped haircut, suggested an Easter chick wearing heavy horn-rimmed glasses. Max added, "Andrew Dana, our librarian. Pa saved him from a college job. He really does know a lot about Byron and all that. And of course he orders in all the new books of any interest. The latest ones are always on that table over there. Take your pick whenever. Let's sit down."

As we did so he pressed an electric button in the paneling, and presently two footmen in day jackets came in bearing our trays which they set down before us. Max thanked them and indicated that we would need nothing more and they withdrew. Like Mr Dana, they might have been, for Max, performing dogs in appropriate costumes.

"So many flowers everywhere," I said. "All down the long gallery, and here in the fireplaces."

"My Ma. It is all she thinks of since her difficulty began." I wanted to know what this was but he went right on. "Aren't you an only child?"

"Yes." (I came late to my parents.)

"I almost am. I have a sister but she's much older and lives abroad. I had a younger brother who died at birth. So you see I'm the only one also."

"Have you minded?"

"That means you have."

"Yes, sometimes."

"Not really," he said. "The chief bother is in having to make up your mind whom to love, instead of loving them before you know it, just by living with them. You know?"

"I haven't thought about it."

"But you think quite deliberately much of the time, don't you, Richie? Does anyone else call you Richie? If they do, I'll think of something else."

"No, they don't. I wish I really could think. Sometimes I think I have nothing up here to do it with."

He laughed while chewing. He ate in big bites and frank appetite.

"I had a time like that. Or rather, everything I made up my mind about immediately suggested the very opposite, and I would switch over to believing *that*."

"How did you settle it?"

"It cleared up by itself when I began to drink and sleep with girls." But he gave me a keen look to see if I believed this.

"Oh."

"Not that we're going to talk about that"—for he had seen in his quick pale glance that it was what I most wanted to hear about, and he never made his gifts in response to what was actually wanted. "I think you might plan to come in here tomorrow morning and look around. Either Mr Dana or my father can show you things. A nice way to have a quiet Fourth of July."

"Will you be busy?"

"I never know. Anyway, I don't know much about all this." This remark was an affectation, as I knew later.

We finished our trays more or less in silence and great speed, Max setting the pace. With a nod he led me out of the library and out of the house. The Isotta was waiting at the front door. The engine was running. His negligences, then, were rules, and he had the power to impose them.

"Do you want to drive?" he asked.

"Thanks, no. I've never driven anything like this, and I didn't bring my license."

"Nonsense. Get in. I'll tell you what to do."

I obeyed and under his coaching the superb car moved off down the hill toward the meadows. I drove carefully. Those were fairly early days of motoring, and the first great cars had wonder built into them. I felt a faintly choked emotion as I handled the big polished steering wheel of striated wood. Manhood spoke to me in my belly and groin with the kind of joy that dreams could bring. Max leaned around to look directly at me. If I had been aching to drive, he would not have been so willing; but seeing my delight, after my hesitancy, he felt like someone who has created something new, out of the most immalleable of elements, which were those of human desire.

"How about it, Richie?" he asked in a soft, intense sound that carried shivers of indefinable intimacy with it. "How about it, boy? Eh?" He ground his admirable teeth together gently, moving his jaw as if in recollection of ultimate pleasure. "Give her the gun, we've got a good straight stretch just over this hill. I'll tell you when to slow down. Gun it, Cousin! You're doing fine!"

The humid air flew past us. He rode leaning forward. His eyes were half closed by a suspended smile. His hands were knotted between his thighs. Tensely he gave himself to sensation. I remember thinking how interesting and strange it was for anyone to find sensual pleasure in speeding by motorcar, for that is just what his fine face and head, with bronze hair modeled by the wind, seemed to show. It was not long until I knew that he met every physical sensation in the same spirit.

※ ※ ※

He showed me the way around the entire Chittenden barony—his father's own place, and the estates of his uncles and cousins. Either on hilltops or sweepingly revealed at the far end of a fold of hills, the family houses presided over the landscape. We returned to Newstead by a back road. About two miles from the house we came alongside a glass structure like a municipal palace of horticulture. This was what it was—"Ma's greenhouse," Max said. It was clearly more than that, for it had broad terraces on its long side facing the valley, where tables and chairs and other furniture, including a fountain set slightly lower on the slope, proposed social events. I could see tall tropical trees inside the towering glass vault of the building.

"We used to have parties there, and concerts," said Max. "All that we do now is the Fourth of July fireworks party every year. You'll see it tomorrow night. We ask a hundred people who come and sit there"—the terrace—"and all the country people from miles around come and sprawl all over the hills where they can see just as well. We're having a dance with it this year, presumably because Marietta and I would like it."

"Won't you?"

"Would you?"

"Why not?"

"Complete with peasants and operatic villagers in the respectful middle distance?"

"But I thought you didn't mind servants and—and—"

"And being rich? I don't, up close. But it's when you back off and look that it seems idiotic. Are your people rich?"

"Not like this. Not anything like it. We have only a cook and one car and we go away in the summer. You can *stay home* every summer."

He laughed at my statement of terms.

"Well, nobody is supposed to talk about it, so I won't. We're supposed to look satisfied and pretend that everybody else lives exactly the way we do, even our poor relations."

"Is that what I am?" I asked, somewhat irritably.

"Would you rather be me?" he asked suddenly without his bantering indifference.

Yes, I said to myself, I would, and at that time it was still true, but before I would say so, I would cut my tongue out. I didn't answer. He leaned and gazed at me. We were still driving and he put a hand on the wheel as if to change my aim. He said,

"Would you? Why can't you tell me. I want to know."

It was like being asked if I loved him. I had no idea about that, but his urgency, the blaze in his eyes, his swift descent into intimacy, paralyzed my thought and word, and I drove on past my Cousin Alicia's botanical garden in silence.

In a moment Max slumped back in his seat and said,

"Well, good for you, Richie. You took a risk and it came out all right. I can respect that."

Risk? I wondered. But now I know what it was and why he admired my silence.

❈ ❈ ❈

Below the last hill near the house we saw the tennis house and courts. Just beyond was a swimming pool with a colonnaded bathhouse.

"How about a couple of sets of singles?" asked Max. "But you didn't bring a racquet."

"No. I did not suppose anyone here played seriously."

He blurted a laugh and said,

"You're picking up our style fast, to say a thing like that. —How do you know I don't play tennis seriously? I suppose you do?"

"Yes. It is the only sport I'm any good at."

"Let's stop. I can lend you everything."

We played. It was mid-afternoon. I was soon running with sweat. He played hard and well but I took the first set six-three. As we changed courts Max paused at the net and gave me a droll smile shining with the golden light of his sweat. There was a kindly glow of approval in it, and also an edge of disbelief that I had beat him so far. He ran his tongue along his upper lip in a calculating taste of the joy it would be to take the next two sets and leave me in my proper place. But I was on a good streak of control and I knew it, and his bantering, threatening amusement did not worry me. My father was a fine player and taught me from early years how to make every stroke a completed act of form. Accuracy and power came later, and by the time I was finishing school tennis was the only sport I loved. My best reassurances came from playing. My doubts vanished, my body obeyed me well, the spring and flight of the ball after a beautiful impact in the exact center of the racquet gave me, at that age, one of the examples, perhaps the only one, of perfect satisfaction in a personal action. All of me went into each stroke, and each seemed for its own sake absolutely worth-while at the instant. What did it matter that afterwards I remembered that it was only a game, and the outcome could not possibly be of any importance? I was fulfilled and delivered whenever I played as well as I knew how to. My pleasure never lasted long; I wished I knew how to gain the same feeling and confirmation from something in life that mattered.

"I'll be God damned," said Max at the end of the second quick set which I took six-love. He stood with his hands on his hips, one leg negligently thrust forward while he examined me from a distance of ten feet as though I were a new species. "Where did you ever learn to play like that? Do you know something? I haven't been beaten for two years. I'd never believe it, looking at you." If now he admired me his candor made it plain that he had not really admired me earlier.

"My father and I have played since I was eight. It doesn't mean anything."

"Anything! Why should it depress you to be so good at tennis?"

"Because even if I am good at it, it doesn't matter at all."

"Oh, yes, by God, it does. You've got to be wonderful at

everything." He shrugged. "At least, that is the law I grew up under, because otherwise my so-called advantages might count for too much." And now he looked at me as if he wished he were I—or so I thought for a moment. The ambiguities in the half-glimpsed awarenesses of young people: what longings struggled to find easement in release, and what poverties of expression stood in the way. Max, not yet quite believing he had been defeated, and on his own court at that, Max, full of some mystified marveling and want, called up such a strong feeling of affinity in me that I suddenly blushed and put my towel up to my streaming face. His tact was equal to the moment.

"Very well," he said, "we need a swim, now, in this heat, after all that."

He led me to the pool. In the little pillared temple at one end we found dressing rooms and showers.

In the water he was like a dolphin streaked with light. In that element he excelled me and was glad of it. He led me in dives which I executed awkwardly. He raced me two lengths and won by half a length. We cooled off and dried and dressed.

"I would think if you can play such good tennis you also might be a good swimmer," he murmured as we sat down on canvas-cushioned long chairs in the shade of the porch.

"I know, it is odd, but I have always been a little uneasy in the water, ever since I can remember."

"That explains it. I suppose someone threw you in when you were too young, leaving you to fight your way to survival, which you did. But ever since, you have thought of swimming as dangerous, which it isn't, really."

I was astonished.

"That is exactly what happened and what it did," I said.

"My father had me taken to the Dorchester Club on Saturday mornings to learn to swim in the pool. The instructor, an old man named Mr Mac, felt how timid I was right away, and saying he would keep an eye on me, he threw me up in the air and into the water. I nearly drowned. An older boy pulled me out. Mr Mac was dismissed. I didn't go back to the water for two years. Even now when I open my eyes under water I feel a little panic."

"You have not yet taken complete command of your whole environment," said Max.

This struck me as a magisterial statement. How could three years of age make so great a difference in the possession of wisdom? For I never considered that there might be more than a difference of age to explain his power and glory. We are told the young learn best through emulation. I intended to return to Dorchester in complete command of my whole environment as a new Maximilian. They would not know me, at home. They would look at me in wonder and think about it before addressing me.

"How do you get command of your whole environment?" I asked.

"The minute you decide it is true, it will be," he replied. "Most people never stop to think of it. —Let's go on up. It is going to rain. You can finish your letter. I am going to go to sleep for a while. I'll come get you when it's time to go for Marietta."

She was thin and small, but she hung heavy like inert matter in my touch as we danced. One flat white arm lay on my shoulder. With the other she dragged my hand down. In her continuing touch I felt an unceasing tremulous energy, a force over which she seemed to have no control. Her color was ghostly, so insubstantial did she look, while her power was frankly physical in how she moved and spoke. Her pale hair was long and loose, cut in a bang across her forehead. Under this her eyes were set in a permanent scowl which seemed to be the prediction of an unsuppressible smile. Trapped light came out in her gaze, which was deep in the shadow of her brow, and heavy shadows smudged the white under her eyes. She wore no make-up but lipstick, in a pale rose color. Her knee-length flat evening frock, in the period style with glass beads scattered over it, hung on her inertly and added its weight to her air of exhaustion. We rocked and stepped against the music of the college-boy dance band, as it was her will to counter her surroundings even in trivial ways. She pressed her lips together as though to deny them the smile which they were made for. Shaking invisibly in my grasp, she made me feel responsible for her, and turning her head away when I said something so that she would be able to control an impulse to laugh hysterically, she delighted me. Her fragrance was heavy, something like the air outside, which since nightfall had been hanging densely in a threat of warm rain. As we moved past the tall open doors of the Glenmere Hunt Club, where we were dining and dancing, I could see fireflies weaving their texture of tiny lights all across the broad meadow below. Max had danced with her once and then given her to me and disappeared.

"He makes me feel married," she said.

"How?"

"Handing me over and going off like that. Husbands hate to look responsible."

"He said you grew up together."

"We did. I nearly killed him once."

"How."

"How, how, how. It is your best word, isn't it?"

"How?" I said.

"You see?"

I had made a poor joke, but she was right, and all my sense was in one or another way given to the question "How?" as I reached to understand anything at all in that year of my life. Childhood had been so sure. She felt that she had reached one of my private vulnerabilities, and her secret little engine shook her until I felt it, and then she said,

"There's so much I could tell you."

"I hope you will."

"No, I mean, it would take a long time. —Come back next summer, will you?"

"I haven't even gone yet."

She made a breathy little groan, and said,

"NGod, I never say the thing I think I'm going to. You don't know how awful it is."

"You said you almost killed Max."

"That. I mean I tried to. It wasn't even an accident. He was seven and I was five, and I got furious because he said I could not be the queen. He was the king and he said if he needed to have a queen he would let me know but so far he did not need one. It was in my playroom on a rainy day and there was a fire in the fireplace. Max was wearing a long royal robe of red crêpe paper. I took a long match from the

[25]

hearth and I lit it in the fire and I set fire to his cape. He watched me do all this, refusing to be bothered or to make me stop, which made me wild. The match caught, and in a second, the king's robe was all flame. It reached up and burned the hair off the back of his head and set fire to his gold paper crown. It went so fast it burned itself out as fast, and didn't light his real clothes. If it had he would have burned up. I ran away crying. He didn't mind my trying to burn him to death, but he told me later I should never run away crying. They had the doctor for him who said he was all right. After he heard that, Max acted frightened for the first time, thinking about what might have happened."

"Were you punished?"

"Nobody ever knew that I did it."

"He didn't tell?"

"No. I did, but nobody believed me, and when they asked him, he said no. I wanted a scandal, but he wouldn't give it to me. Isn't he dreadful?"

"But you became friends again."

"I said I would never forgive him, but he said I would sooner or later. I don't think I ever have, but then."

She lifted and then slumped in my grasp, and gave me one of her sudden direct glances, and through her general air of suppressions, I saw glee and mischief, as well as some suggestion of extraordinary strength, contained within her exhausted air and her little shaking indirectness.

"But then what?" I asked.

"But then we are engaged, though not publicly. A few people are supposed to be told about it tomorrow night at Newstead. A ball. Fireworks. Promise to dance with me. He won't, and nobody else will."

We moved along in silence for a few vaguely walked

steps, and then I said, feeling I had been accepted within her world,

"Yes, I want to. Thank you."

"NGod, how polite all you people from places like Dorchester are."

In a word she put me outside again, after I had been forgetfully comfortable.

"—Oh, I didn't mean it that way," she said, for her little throbbing bones told her what I felt. "I only mean—oh, it's so awful, never to be like what you want to be, I mean, we are all so ghastly around here, we are rude and we say anything we think of no matter what, and I mean, I loved it when you said thank you. I mean Dorchester must be divine, if they are all like you. You know. Like that. Richard," she ended, making somewhere behind her nose a comic groan out of my name, "if you want to stop dancing with me this minute we can go and sit down and stare at our empty plates till Max comes back."

"Will he come back?"

"Oh, yes. He always does." She gave a breath of a laugh through her nostrils and said, "I suppose it is the best I can ever hope for."

"No, let's dance till the music stops."

It stopped just then on an unresolved chord.

"There he is," she said.

She pointed. Max was at the orchestra platform, talking to the youth who led the band from his piano bench. In another moment, Max was coming toward us.

"Do you begin to see Max?" she asked. "Who else would stop the band just to make us stop dancing?"

"Did he? Is that why?"

"Oh, yes, he did, it is."

Max came to us and stepped between us. He took us each by an arm and led us away.

"We have all had enough of this dreariness, don't you think?" he asked.

"But we were going to dance until I wore holes in my fine slippers," said Marietta.

"I know. But I am ready to go."

"You've been drinking," she said.

"Yes. Do you want a drink?"

"We all do."

"I have a bottle in the car"—the Prohibition style.

"It is beginning to rain."

"Yes. We'll get wet."

"Oh, lovely."

We found Marietta's little evening coat of flimsy gold India silk and we all went out into the rain. She put her coat up over her head and ran with us to the car.

"Are you going to put up the top?" asked Marietta.

"No," replied Max, opening the car door for her. The deep leather seat was slick with rain. We sat together and drank from a bottle of Canadian rye whiskey which Max brought out and then he started the car and turned on the great headlamps. Raindrops fell like pellets of gold in the long shafts of light we threw ahead. We rode soaking wet along the hilly roads, drinking as often as Max felt like it, and shivering in the air which we stirred by our speed, while the warm rain fell heavily. We were mostly silent. Once or twice Max looked past Marietta at me to see how I regarded the mournfully perverse episode, and something told me to show no feeling. I gazed back at him blankly, and then turned away. I was seized by baffled admiration, and I was also aware of a resentment which I knew to be unworthy of my membership in the league of those who rode around for hours in pouring rain with no protection; a resentment which I could not suppress; for I was wearing the only clothes I had brought in which to dress up in the evening, and they were now ruined. My cousin could find himself other things to wear, but I could not. The gallantry of the adventure was for me mixed with the misery of a country cousin who can never hope to meet the affluent and grand on their own terms. But—so anguished and proud are the young—it was impossible for me to show my honest concern over such a matter, and the Canadian whiskey kept me from recognizing the pathos of the drenched merry-making into which Max took us in darkness, torrent, and puddle, with nowhere really to go.

❧ ❧ ❧

"My dear Richard," said the note in the smallest hand-writing I have ever seen, "they tell me you are here. Welcome. We are always curious to see the next generation. Maximilian has a notion that you would like to look about the library. Unless he has mysterious and complicated plans for you, would you care to join me at ten o'clock in the library and let me show you a few pieces in the collection? Mr Dana is coming to work with me at ten-forty-five, but until then I shall be pleased to see you. I am afraid that may be our only chance, as the day will be busy, and you are to leave us, I'm afraid, on the sixth, and I alas must be in Philadelphia on the fifth.

Alexander Chittenden."

It was addressed to me with "Esqre." after my name—the first time I had ever been given the title. The envelope was on my breakfast tray which was brought to my sitting room. My first response to the note was to think that an extremely small man must have written it—someone to match the scale of the minute script. But as I discovered later, I was wrong. My Cousin Alexander was very tall and lean, with a small protuberant belly under his unaccented black suit. I had never seen a photograph of him, but when I actually met him, he made me think of a photograph, for all his colors were in values of gray and white and black. His eyes were black, set, like his son's, under dark porches, but their light had been long extinguished by I knew not what. Over them he wore large, perfectly round spectacles, in frames of the thinnest gold. His face was narrow and pale, with deep downward lines about the mouth. His hands were long, white, and moist; they held to each other much of the time. When he moved it was with a strange, angular animation, almost like gaiety, with wide swings of his narrow shoulders and stylish strides of his long legs. He was almost bald, with a few streaks of still dark hair brushed flat across his head. A long-linked gold watch chain across his waistcoat made an accent of light in his general dark. In no way, except perhaps in the trait of character or habit of command which led him to limit the terms of our meeting and my visit, did he remind me of Max. I thought his note a trifle unnecessarily cautious about when I must leave him and I did not think it wonderfully polite that he reminded me of the day I was expected to depart. I daydreamed for a moment of the luxury it would be to send another note back—"Dear Cousin Alexander, how good of you to suggest a visit to the library, but actually, I have other plans for the morning, and in fact, it may be that I will have to leave a day earlier than I had planned. Perhaps another time. If you are ever in Dorchester, do call us. I am sure my parents would be pleased to see you, even if I should happen to be engaged. With regrets and thanks for my visit to Newstead, which I find a very pleasant place, I am Yours faithfully"— but the bridling, precocious rudeness of this was soon lost like any dream, and when the valet came to take away my tray, I was dressing for ten o'clock.

"Is my Cousin Max done with his breakfast?" I asked.

"No, sir. He is sleeping. We are not to call him before twelve."

"Oh. I see. Oh—my suit got soaked through last night—I wonder if there is any way you could help with—"

"I have it now, sir. It is still damp, but we're drying it out and it will be pressed and ready for you before this evening."

I thanked him, wondering if I should ask him whether it had shrunk. He nodded cheerfully at me, almost with a wink, which could mean either that he was a young pink-faced Irishman naturally agreeable, or that he saw through my unaccustomed air of ease to my real concern as a young man with only one suit on a visit to another world.

"Yes, sir. It will be very grand this evening, with the music and the fireworks. You didn't bring a dinner jacket, sir?"

"Oh, no. Will they wear them tonight?"

"Oh, yes, sir. The invited people will all dress."

The possibility had never occurred to any of us in Dorchester, for youths my age did not possess evening clothes, even though my father and mother put on their special finery several times a week during the winters.

"But I'm sure your blue suit will do very well, sir."

"It will have to," I said bitterly, full of regret that I had come.

"Unless you could use one of Mr Max's, sir? You're a trifle taller, but we could let down the braces and 'twould never be noticed."

How to decide which would be the distinguished thing to do—to borrow a dinner jacket carelessly, or smile with forgiveness upon those who thought it mattered how one dressed for a formal dinner dance followed by a fireworks concert in Chittenden Hills? A phrase came to my rescue from the tone of family councils at home when a decision of some importance was hovering over us unresolved.

"Thank you," I said, "we'll see."

"Of course, sir. Thank you, sir."

He took away my tray from which at the last instant I rescued the note. I felt deeply unhappy; and I thought I had felt so ever since my arrival. I could not say why, in particular, but the general feeling of the whole place, the persons and the events in whose midst I found myself, seemed to me so alien that I had a gulping wave of homesickness, though I refused to give it that name even in my thoughts, for if I had made conscious the word, I would have had to admit that what I was homesick for was my childhood, when I was the center of all events and concerns, and when it was I who made the laws within certain conventions which were acceptable as they were devised for my welfare, and when my view of the world was lovely to those who saw it with me.

❧ ❧ ❧

The library doors were open on a deep avenue of rich shadow where symmetrical pools of golden light shone down the room. As I appeared in the doorway,

"Yes, do come in, how nice," said Alexander Chittenden in a voice of high register which seemed to issue through a whole crosshatching of scratches until it sounded like an old Victrola record.

He walked from the farthest golden pool to meet me, swaying through long strides with a sort of prim elegance. He took my hand without grasping it. His touch was cold. He looked at his watch to see whether I had come precisely at ten, and since I had, he put it back into his waistcoat pocket saying,

"Oh, good." His pronunciation was sandily precise, with little special effects which I thought of as belonging to his caste—that of the few millionaires in the country whose wealth had come down through several generations of severe education and ingrown style. I won't try to sustain a phonetic rendering of this, but an occasional example or two might bring him more sharply to mind. He said "wirld" for "world," and he lengthened certain vowels fastidiously. When he meant "girl" he said "geel," and "pearl" came out "pirl," and "first" was "feest." Now he said, "Well, feest, Richard, as I shall call you, and as we are remote cousins by mahrriage, I do think it abseed if we say Mister to me, don't you: and yet Cousin Alexander seems odd, too, don't we think? At owah difference in age and the rest? I have thought we would settle on Uncle Alec for me, and Ahnt Lissy for my wife. You do think so?"

My father had said with comic awe that Alexander Chittenden was supposed to be worth upwards of four hundred million dollars, and he had added, "Poor fellow." "Poor fellow?" said my mother with charming scorn, "I could bear it if you were as poor as that. I cannot find it necessary to pity Lissy and Alec." "Yes," said my father, "think of having to work hard to be like other people." I had been mystified by this at the time, but now I remembered it, and I saw that Uncle Alec did work hard to be friendly and easy, like other people, but I saw too that he failed, since his idea of what other people were like, as it showed in him, was like nothing I had ever known. If he was rather a caricature, he seemed to make people he encountered into caricatures also.

"How kind of you to come to be with my son," he said. "There is no one to amuse him here. I am shaw you chaps are going to have a bully time togethah. I do hope you'll come agane."

Brightly scratched forth, this remark like his note carried hints of dismissal but now it was clear that he was anticipating my departure with regret and so must hasten to absorb it as an accepted fact.

"Thank you. Perhaps I can."

"But do let's get to wirk," he said, "as the librarian will soon be here with some new catalogues. —Do you care for Lord Byron and his period?"

"I don't know much about it."

"How very good. Then I can tell you the little I know—" and satisfaction leaked through the scratches of his throat, and he took me to the grilled and locked shelves and began what was a set-piece which he always enjoyed giving for visitors, whether scholars or schoolboys.

We began with a complete flight, as he called it, of feest

editions of all the known wirks of Byron. As he told me about them, he took down an occasional volume. Thinking he meant to hand it to me, I reached for it, but he didn't notice, but kept hold of the book, turning a few pages delicately with his long middle finger, and lingering over the paper with the lightest of touches. He was able to point out which volumes had been gathered by his father and which by himself, for it appeared that he had taken the collection much farther toward uniqueness and completeness than the founder of it. He said the delight in collecting was to reconstruct a whole life through the scattered items brought together in such a place as this. From complete first editions we moved on to special editions and then to single volumes of interest. I remember his pleasure in showing me but not handing to me several volumes of Byron which bore Shelley's autograph in the flyleaves. Others had belonged to Leigh Hunt. There was one rather smudged volume signed "Claire" on the title page, and in margins of later pages it bore exclamation points, question marks, dots, and wavy lines alongside various passages which for reasons never to be known had arrested the attention, and possibly the pathetic feelings, of Byron's discharged mistress. As he showed me these Uncle Alec's long dry cheeks glowed faintly with a little color, and he said to me with careful restraint, most becoming to an elder who speaks of risky matters to a youth,

"They were lovers, as you know. She bore his child—a daughter. He treated her badly—" and at this, restraint gave way to withdrawal of his lips in what was surely a smile of relish which could not be suppressed. But a sudden dry, cracking sound from somewhere in the great room made him look up and about with a drawn frown. "What on eeth was that!"

"I don't know—it sounded like a piece of wood breaking."

"It couldn't have been. How disagreeable. —I cannot *stand* unexplained noises," he said irritably, yet with a hint of shame at his distress. He put up a finger to hold silence until we should hear the noise again. It did not come. Presently he aroused himself, snapped poor Claire Clairemont's book shut and replaced it, and with it, put out of sight and mind the excitement that had begun to show in him at the idea of treating a mistress badly. He unlocked a case of deep sliding trays containing manuscripts. These were poems by Byron; those were by Shelley; here was a sheaf of letters by Trelawney —"uttah cad, yet somehow fascinating"; some essays by Godwin in brown ink on blue paper, tied with yellowed muslin tape; and here—"a most precious piece, for I found it myself, in of all places Brighton, in a peefectly commonplace tourist antique shop, and I had it out of there in five minutes for one pound seven shillings, and dealers have since made me preposterous offers for it, but one of them had overlooked it a week before, for he told me so!" Uncle Alec was wanly alight with the renewed joy of his bargain and the fruits of his own expertness in which no dealer had served him. The item was a letter written by Edward Bulwer-Lytton from Brocket, where as a youthful beau who reminded some people of Lord Byron himself when young, he was staying with Lady Caroline Lamb in her sequestration and dotty misery. You see, explained Uncle Alec, she had had that wild affair with Byron, it ended in hatred and bitterness, and yet she could not uproot him from her heart, and she used to send for young Bulwer-Lytton to come and play the organ for her and she would stare at him remembering Byron. His cheeks began to flush again with a hectic grayish orange stain below the skin. Ah me, he murmured more to himself than to me, returning the letter to its case, if one looked long enough, in the right places, with the right questions, one could find almost all there was to know about any lives of long ago. He touched a first edition of *Glenarvon* by Caroline Lamb saying that it was a positive beehive of the bitterest honey in the account it gave of her affair with Byron.

"Where to stop?" he suddenly asked with a widened smile of proprietary pleasure. "Yes, for example, this d'licious item."

He took down a blue morocco case, opened its elegantly fitted little door, and from an inner folder drew out a thick pile of pages which crackled under his touch.

"Have you the faintest idea what this is?" he asked.

I shook my head.

"For ever so long it was believed lost and destroyed. Byron mentions it to his little friend Miss Pigot in a letter he wrote from Trinity, at Cambridge. I remember the exact words. 'I have written 214 pages of a novel,' he wrote. Every young man writes a novel, I daresay you have done so yourself, Richard? —Ha. I thought so. —Yes. Well. But this is Byron's. We found it through the most killing coincidences which I have promised not to tell. Scholars long to publish it; but again I have promised not to let them. Meantime, think of it: I have read it, quite idiotic and fascinating, you know, ruins by moonlight, mad heiresses, that sort of thing, you know, doomed heroes, though nobody knows why the doom. But how *readable*: his supreme gift. The letters: Max loves the letters, too. He pores over them, copies out bits of them. I recommend them as a book to travel with."

He replaced the manuscript and we went on.

The collection took in Byron, all his friends, all his places, all his available memorabilia—"if you like locks of hair, we have one"—and of course the requirement was to possess only manuscripts, first editions, association editions with clear evidence either attached or inscribed, and objects authenticated by certified credentials. Take the Thorwaldsen bust on the pedestal, there: it was one of two, the other being in the Murray collection. This one was a secret copy. It was a rather vulgar thing, no life in it, but it had to be had, once you knew it was available. Authentic duplicates, if you could call them that, were peefectly legitimate. Here was another —in a narrow glass case on thin table legs, on a blue velvet bed, and lighted from within the glass, was a long saber in its scabbard, wearing a tarnished gold bullion loop and knot on the elaborately chased gold hilt, which Byron had kept at Missolonghi. With other effects it had been brought home to England by Fletcher.

Uncle Alec took a glance at his watch. There was time for only one more item.

"A great treasure of the collection," he said, and moved me to a paneled space between bookshelves where a blue velvet curtain covered the wall. He touched a button, a light came on, he touched another, and the curtains parted to reveal a heavily framed and glassed notebook pencil sketch of a man in profile. His forehead was bald far beyond an expected hairline. His hair was wavy but looked thin against his skull. His face was fleshy about the jowl, which was partially concealed by a black silk neckcloth. The eye was dotted in lightly so that it looked pale. The eyebrow was gallant and firm. Straight and long, the nose was unremarkable above the scrolled lips which held a pout of appetite or doubt. The body, with narrow shoulders, was clothed in a ruffled shirt, waistcoat, and lounging coat. A jeweled stud held the shirt together in front. It was, said my cousin, a drawing of Lord Byron by Count Alfred D'Orsay which had been done at Genoa in 1823. There was another in London which Uncle Alec had seen, but he thought this one, obviously done at the same sitting, much finer. Nobody knew of its existence, permission had never been given to reproduce it, and of all the likenesses of Byron—and they were all here in one form or another—this had always struck Uncle Alec as the one nearest to life, though it had so little real skill.

"Don't you think?"

"But I don't know," I said. "I always thought Lord Byron was handsome."

"So we are told. But everything changes, and of course, he lived recklessly, and did not care how he looked after he left England, and for too long, in any case, he looked like a superb boy. Sometimes I wonder what Maximilian will look like when he is my age?"

Uncle Alec gazed at me soberly through his large circles of clear lens. I think he was looking through my youth at his own before life had drained away his color and sent his passions to sleep. I had a stir of pity for a moment, and then a little chill of dislike, though whether for him or for what life must do to everyone, I did not know. He closed the curtain and shut off the light.

"What," he asked, in the dry manner of a teacher administering the Regents' Examination, "what words of Byron's do you think you will never forget?"

"Oh, I think *There was a sound of revelry by night,*" I replied.

"Yes, most people would I think give that. But the one phrase I think has all of him in it is this one, also from

Childe Harold." He paused, and then in a much reduced voice so that the scratches almost drowned out the words, he said, *"The late remorse of love."*

He gave me a bleak look, somewhat like that of an animal pet in a moment of shamed regret for some pathetic transgression. On that morning that phrase of Byron held no such meaning for me as that which muted Uncle Alec; but now I know that "the late remorse of love" needs a lifetime for its resonance to echo in the heart.

The spill of morning light from the main gallery was cut and shafted by the small alert entrance of the librarian, exactly on time at a quarter before eleven.

His employer greeted him with relief, I was introduced, and Uncle Alec said,

"Do browse when you have a moment, Richard. There are many books of interest which are not kept locked. The lib'ry is usually unoccupied between two and four. Mr Dana will be happy to help you."

Mr Dana cringed agreeably in silence to support this offer of his services.

"Now what did you bring for me?" asked Uncle Alec, and without further ceremony, he and Mr Dana escorted the acquisitive instinct to the librarian's corner at the far end of the room.

❋ ❋ ❋

Air, I said to myself without using the word, and I went to the great front door of Newstead and let myself out. The driveway with its sickle curve of white marble chips looked hot in the hazy morning. I walked down the avenue of hemlocks that attached the hilltop to the valley below. I felt that too much from a dead life had been laid upon me too quickly. I felt cross at Max for not being awake and about, so I could talk to him or play tennis. The hum of summer sounded above the rolling meadows—or else in my inmost ear. I heard another sound—the busy, cupping clops of a horse walking, and around a curve between the hemlocks came Marietta riding a tall and shining mare the color of a violin. When she saw me she broke into a trot and posted up to me, halted, and sat smiling at the ground beyond me. She wore jodhpurs and short boots, a silk blouse, and a starched stock with a gold safety pin thrust through it.

"Did you ever dry out?" she asked.

"I'm as dusty as a mummy," I answered.

"You've been in the library."

"Just now."

"Where shall we go?"

"Do you want to go somewhere?"

"I thought we would."

"But you're riding."

She dismounted and took the bridle over the head to lead her horse.

"There's a gate just there. We'll go in the meadow. I know a little brook. My tall friend here can have a nice graze."

"Max is asleep."

"I know. I telephoned to ask you both to ride with me. They told me he was not to be called and that you were with Alexander."

"Do you call him that?" I asked.

"No. Just to myself. God knows what I'll call him when I'm married. —What do you call him?"

"He told me to call him Uncle Alec, though really we are cousins."

She made one of her painfully suppressed smiles as if her amusement at everything, or fondness for me, were simply too intense to be allowed out, and said,

"I adore people who tell other people what to call them. It's like making them use a flattering nickname for you which you made up for yourself, because what other people might make up would be awful. —We can stretch out here."

There was a small sky-rippling brook between tall grasses and wild flowers. An immense old oak tree stood a little away but its shadow was so commodious that it took us in. Marietta was pale, her eyes were hooded by shadows beneath the delicate skin. I saw her little wrists and arms. She appeared more fragile in the summer daylight than she had the night before. She suddenly looked at me directly, as she so rarely did.

"I know how you feel," she said.

"You do?"—wondering myself really how I felt.

"Yes," and she told me.

※ ※ ※

So alien, she said. She had grown up here and yet there were days when even she felt unreal with the Chittendens, or, in self-preservation, had to conclude that they were unreal.

"Oh, dear," she said. "Other people must be simple in lots of things. Why can't we be? Can you help me? Or all of us? Or any of us?"

"Lord. I don't know."

But she gazed at me again, as if I were a doctor or a priest; and then at my perplexity she laughed and reached out and took my near hand and turned it palm upward, pushed my cuff back to expose my inner wrist, and began lightly, with the touch of a butterfly, to stroke the skin where my blue veins showed through and my pulse made its tiny vital lump every second.

"Doesn't it feel lovely?" she asked.

"Oh, yes."

"Do mine."

She gave me her wrist and I stroked it in the same way.

"Oh, why can't everything be as easy and lovely as this feels, all the time. You are a darling and I love your being bothered all the time. Nobody I know is bothered by anything, except something that never shows, whatever it is. Do you want to kiss me?"

"Yes."

But if she was engaged to my cousin Max perhaps I shouldn't. Before I could decide, she said, drawing a little away,

"No, you are right. I am just lonely."

"That is a good reason to be kissed."

"I think you are lonely too."

"Sometimes."

"Why?"

"I don't know."

"No, but I know why I am," she said. She picked a few wild flowers that grew between us where we reclined on the damp earth which still smelled of last night's rain. She began to twine the stems together making a small wreath. It became a bracelet which she slipped over her white narrow hand to her wrist.

"But you ought not to be lonely if you are in love with Max."

"Oh, you sweet Richard, that is just why. —What do you think of him?"

"Oh, he is—" and I remembered how I went on to describe him in my letter to my parents, and more. I saw his ample air, his fine looks, his sudden absences even while he was right with you, his unconscious sense of privilege, his ability to laugh at himself, and his preference for disorder over the dead calm order of the domestic life all about him. I had to admit that I was surprised that he slept the morning away.

"Does he always sleep all morning?" I asked.

"He wakes up early and he telephones me and we talk. We talked half an hour about you this morning. Then he often goes back to sleep. But he doesn't really sleep. He reads, or thinks lying down, or simply exists, as he says. He says he has a great desire for privacy."

This seemed striking in a youth, and I recognized something of myself in him, or of my daydreams about myself, and not for the first time since the day before.

"He asked me if I minded being an only child. He said he felt like one, though actually he isn't."

"No. His sister. She lives in Venice. She married an Italian and made a scandal."

"Really? A scandal?"

"Yes. She became a Catholic."

"Oh. Is that a scandal here?"

"Oh, yes."

"I am a Catholic."

"We know that."

"But it doesn't matter, outside, you mean?"

"Something like that. —Don't be troubled. It only matters to Alexander and Alicia. Not to me or Max. —What do you think matters to Max?"

"Let me see. I think what matters to him," I said carefully, feeling worldly and penetrating, as I rarely did, "is to have everybody think he is the most fortunate and happy man in the world, and most people do, but sometimes he forgets how to have them think so, and then something else matters, but I don't know what."

She leaned and swiftly and lightly kissed my cheek and then sat away and looked down the long meadow toward the pretty barriers of the paddock and said,

"When he is sure of anyone, he doesn't try any further. It doesn't mean he doesn't want them, just the same. Do you know what first made us stop thinking of each other as children—playmates?"

"No?"

"It was the day I saw him suffer for the first time. I think perhaps my heart—probably anyone's—is made of something like a wishbone in a bird. Because that day when I saw him I felt something go crack right here exactly like a wishbone when we pulled it in the nursery"—her hand at her breast—"and it was for him."

"What happened to make something break like that?"

When Maximilian was seventeen, four years ago: my own age in the summer in the meadow with Marietta—he was stricken with a responsibility of the heart which was like a watershed in the inner landscape of his life. In fact, it was so great that his father Alexander could not meet it. Someone of the family had to do it and Max was the only one they thought of.

His mother was then, everyone said, still wonderfully beautiful. Max was very close to her. He was supposed to look like her. Nobody ever saw any trace of his father in him. Everyone decided this with hidden relief, for Alexander Chittenden, aside from his fortune, for years had had little about him which interested other people, and it seemed to them that he was quite satisfied that this be so. The one person he cared for—his daughter—had gone away long ago. He settled a great dowry upon her, forgave her formally for her desertion, and for her marrying an Italian of title, and for her conversion. With the boyhood of his other child he had little connection thereafter. His wife was absorbed in Maximilian's life, though she kept their love for each other in place with a playful etiquette of miniature formalities. Amidst the magnificence and profusion into which she had married, quite unlike the terms of her own early life, she held herself like a reigning consort. Her enthusiasms were real though controlled, and she worked devotedly for every good cause in the countryside and the large cities beyond. She loved flowers, and had developed a charming talent for painting them in still life. All year she worked at her pictures and by Christmas her gift problem was plentifully solved; for, as everyone knew, she could buy anything at all to give away, and therefore a purchased gift seemed meaningless, so the best possible evidence of her fondness was to give something she herself had spent loving hours upon. In the evenings, friends would see with pleasure and amusement that a faint stain of pigment in the fingers of her right hand might remain after the morning's work in her studio, and they would ask what she was working on, and she would answer, "Oh, one of my eighteenth-century floral excesses, I am quite out of fashion, you know."

She tried to get Max to draw, but he had no talent. He did better at writing, and his letters from school and college were careless, irregular in their sequence, and often wickedly outspoken; but they had him there right on the page, and she read and reread and kept them all.

"We all did. I did," said Marietta. "His very voice is on the paper. He was the most high-spirited—nobody could really describe what he was like. His mother and I used to trade his letters and then meet to talk about them. She adored him more than he ever knew. —Oh, the *thingness* of everything!"

"Everything?"

"You'll see. —Now he looks at everyone as if he would find in their faces something he has to know."

Then in his last year at school, as I was now, he was suddenly summoned home. Marietta was staying at home that year working with a tutor. Her father, the physician, was in charge at Newstead, and it was he who had asked for Max to return. Having called in surgeons in consultation, he had grave news for Max about both his mother and his father. Marietta remembered all of it, in detail.

Mrs Chittenden had felt a throbbing inflammation in a

finger of her right hand, but not believing in self-indulgence she ignored it for several days. Only when holding a brush became awkward and painful did she ring up her neighbor Doctor Osborne to ask him what to do for an infection surrounding a fingernail. (There was a name for it which Marietta could not remember.) The doctor declared that he should see it. He recognized what it was, said it must be lanced, drained, and watched rather closely to be sure it did not persist, as those things often did. He looked further to discover whether the inflammation might have spread through the blood vessels of the hand and forearm.

Marietta took my arm again, but not this time for tender play, but to show what she knew of the doctor's next discovery.

"There," she said, pressing a spot above my wrist on the inner surface of my arm. "There was a strange sort of lump or swelling in her arm. He asked her how long she had had it, and she said that she had noticed it, but had thought nothing of it. She asked if it had anything to do with the finger."

Doctor Osborne thought not. Had she bruised her arm in any way? She could not remember. He treated the finger, bandaged it, and asked her if she would go into Philadelphia the next day to see a certain surgeon, and if advised to do so, whether she would consent to have x-rays taken of the arm swelling.

Mrs Chittenden asked him what he was thinking of, and he told her. It was by no means a certainty, but under any such possibility as this swelling suggested, it was sensible to take every precaution without delay. She had a certain look, said Marietta, which she used when there was any occasion for understanding beyond words. Doctor Osborne received that look now. They were old friends. He nodded.

Some days later he had the report from Philadelphia. The x-rays revealed nothing definitive. However, Doctor de Kranowitz, the Philadelphia surgeon, recognized certain suggestive symptoms, and advised an immediate surgical exploration. Doctor Osborne examined Mrs Chittenden again, and found changes in the arm. He talked the case over with Doctor de Kranowitz by telephone. They agreed that no time should be lost, even though the tumor should prove to be benign, for the risk of the opposite condition was equally present, and in that event they came to conclusions about what would have to be done.

Alexander Chittenden was in Washington, where he served on a committee on war supplies convened by Secretary Newton D. Baker. Doctor Osborne spoke to him on the telephone, advising him to return home at once, before the committee adjourned, and when he reached home, described to him the strange, and possibly grave, condition which had been discovered in his wife.

"Alexander asked what it meant," said Marietta, "and my father had to tell him."

"Tell what."

"Tell that if it was the worst, they would have to amputate. They wouldn't know until they actually began the operation."

On hearing this, Alexander Chittenden nearly fainted. He was obliged to sit down and lean over, with Doctor Osborne's large, competent hand on the back of his neck.

"What did they do?" I asked.

"They sent for Max."

Max came home within twelve hours. His mother had already been taken to the hospital in Philadelphia. Her husband was of no help to her. Doctor Osborne saw him collapse into the state of querulous terror and inaction which accompanied what was then called "nervous prostration." As head of the family, he had had to be given the technical facts about his wife's forbidding illness. If formal sanction had to be given for the surgeons to proceed in the event of amputation this would be asked of the patient, still, it was of the utmost importance for her psychological state and proper strength of will that she have the loving support of someone close to her. She would have to face a dreadful ordeal, if the worst should come true. Her husband, managing fortunes every year in his office, or giving his dry intelligence and rather low vitality to the wartime disposal of huge resources governing millions of statistical human destinies, met tasks which were within his capacity, for they remained abstractions; it was for such things, said Marietta, that he lived. The possible necessity of maiming a living individual who belonged to him, even though for years only nominally, was an act too concrete for him to face. Doctor Osborne ordered him to bed rest, sent for nurses, and waited for Max.

When Max heard the story he asked, Why hadn't they gone ahead? The doctor replied that in cases of this kind, they would not know how far they must go until they had taken tissue and examined it actually during the operation; and if it should prove to be necessary, then the surgeons would feel easier if they had authorization. Max wanted to know who gave the authorization. Usually, said Doctor Osborne, if the patient was in sound mind, it was the patient. In case the patient was under anesthesia, then he or she would have given someone close by—not a minor—the authority to act. And my mother? asked Max. Does she know? Yes, she knew, and she suggested that her husband be at hand to make the decision if it should be necessary. Well, would he? asked Max. Doctor Osborne hoped so.

Well: what was to be done?

Well: they would try to help Alexander to pull himself together and go to the hospital this afternoon, but it seemed clear that Max must be there to help him to speak for the family if he had to. If the first stage of the operation supported the worst suspicions, the doctors would expect approval in going ahead.

And if this were not given?

Doctor Osborne explained the eventually mortal alternative. He put his hand on Maximilian's shoulder and braced him with affectionate strength. He had delivered Max at birth, and had always been close to him without seeming to be. The touch of sympathy released Max's youthful rage at shocking circumstance. He burst angrily into tears and pounded Doctor Osborne's chest with his forehead. Something terrible might be asked of him. Between his gulping sobs, he muttered bitterly about his father, saying things he had said at various times to Marietta. "My father: he should: he has never: for years he has acted as if he had no blood in his veins: none of us have been quite human in his eyes."

No, no, murmured the doctor, trying to disagree with Maximilian, but without conviction. It was Alicia whom everybody loved, Max most of all, and the doctor told Marietta later that he could quite feel the warmth of Max's love for his mother as they drove through the country and into Philadelphia to the hospital. In the end, Alexander Chittenden was unable to face the endurance awaiting them all at the hospital—Max went alone with Doctor Osborne.

How did it all happen? Max wanted to know.

The doctor said they could not be sure. The more serious difficulty was discovered quite by accident.

Max wanted to know what could have caused that.

"Your mother doesn't remember, but a bruise, a contusion which took its effect quite some time later, may have begun the tumor. We all bump ourselves now and then and do not pay much attention to the hurt, which is usually temporary. Now and then, quite rarely, actually, one of these things develops into something more serious."

Max scowled. A small nudge of memory was working to remind him of something. His face went cold and he glanced sidewise at the doctor, who was driving. A bruise? he said. Yes, some blow on the tender, inner forearm.

Would it matter how long ago this may have happened?

Oh, surely, replied Doctor Osborne. Anything dating from a year or so ago would by now have meant nothing, if symptoms had not appeared earlier. A few months—two to four—would probably show the effect if any were to develop.

"I see," said Max.

"Why?" asked the doctor. Max looked flushed now and at the same time haggard.

"I just remembered."

The doctor nodded and Max told him about something which had happened at the start of the Thanksgiving vacation thirteen weeks ago. Somehow it was easier to tell about it sitting beside the doctor than if they had been facing each other in a room.

One evening there was a rustic party at Newstead, with costumes and country dances, for Max and all his young friends who were home from school for the holiday. Parents attended, loyally dressed up as rubes and hoboes, dairy-maids and pioneer women. There was straw on the floor of the big dairy barn down in the meadow. The family servants were also present. Once a year Alexander Chittenden made it a point to dance with the cook. The climax of the evening was a square dance. Max went as a scarecrow, holding a rusty, broken rake in his torn cotton gloves which had straw sticking out of the finger holes. He kept his rake in the dance and used it grandly to thump the floor in accent with the hired music, which came from a fiddle, an earthenware jug, a bowed saw, a tub (bottom end up), and a set of dented sleighbells on a length of harness strap. The party was animated, for a great vat of hard cider was open to those who felt thirst. In one of the dance figures, the men and women wove in and out of each other's ranks in braided lines. When dancers came to the end of their row, they whirled sharply and dropped hands and with their other hands reached for new partners. It was a pretty gesture which men made with waggery, ladies with comically exaggerated grace. Max dropped the hand of Frazier's wife, whirled energetically holding his rake handle gallantly out, and reached for his new partner. In the same second he saw that it was his mother and that as she reached for him with her right arm her gesture collided with the oaken staff he brandished so recklessly. She exclaimed. He threw away his rake and took her arm to see if he had hurt her. She pressed her lips with pain but shook her head, and then recovering herself, she seized his hand and danced him along after the couple ahead while he stammered his apologies. He suddenly stopped feeling like a joyous scarecrow. She felt the change and shook him gaily, reminding him by her tugging at him that they must always set the spirit of any event of which they were part. Their guests must now not be allowed to notice any mishap or its brief consequences. The fiddle squeaked, the jug pooped, the saw sang, the tub thumped, the sleigh-bells wrangled, and the dance went on. Max never picked up his rake again. He could feel too well the jar and ache of the blow he had given his mother.

He looked aside at Doctor Osborne with inquiry.

"Possibly," mused the doctor. "It is always mysterious."

"Oh, no," said Max, covering his eyes with his hand.

"You mustn't think about it," said the doctor. "There may have been any number of other abrasions—"

There was a silence, and then Max asked,

Will I see her?

Yes, for her sake certainly. For his, too.

Yes, surely, yes—Max looked wild, experiencing in imagination what lay behind and what might lie ahead.

"How do you mean?" I asked.

Marietta crumpled herself together with the effect of shaking off sense and silently asking how it was that you came to know truths which lay beyond words. Then she said,

"He didn't know enough about it to be scientific about it, like my father. But he knew enough about the ghastly idea of it to feel it in his very own bone and flesh. —He always feels everything, all over, on himself, everything he hears about what happens to anyone else. When that thing was coming toward them all, about his mother, he wished it could happen to him instead. But it couldn't. But still there was a ray of hope, and that's what he had to keep thinking in front of all the other feelings—especially the one about the rake at the square dance. But."

Marietta pressed a desperate breath out of her little chest as she remembered more of what she had been told.

At the hospital they went up in an elevator and down a long echoing corridor. Max went alone to his mother. The nurses said she was drowsy but awake. Doctor Osborne waited outside. Max returned to him after ten minutes. He was still wearing the schoolboy smile with which he had greeted his mother, but his face was white as milk, and for a moment he did not want to speak.

Presently he told Doctor Osborne that he had embraced his mother, wanting her to exult in the surprise of his return from school for a few days. She murmured a word of concern that he should miss classes, and he said it did not matter, as his marks were so good he could afford it. He intended to stay around to keep her amused until she was better. She asked where his father was, and he lied enthusiastically, not protecting his father as he was but his wish for the father as he wanted him to be, saying that he was at home, unable to leave, because of long-distance calls from Washington on war business.

Max said she touched his face with her free hand and looked calmly and deeply into his eyes. Did she remember what he had just now revived so vividly during the ride from Newstead to the hospital? He could not imagine asking her. He realized that she knew everything, but he thought she wasn't sure whether he knew everything as well; and to spare him, in case he did not know, she smiled and nodded, he said, and when he saw her do her best to spare him, he had to leave. He bent over and kissed her and came out feeling angry and alone in his guilt. The surgical orderlies passed him on their way to bring his mother to the operating room.

"Do you know?" he said to Marietta afterward, and she never forgot it, "the worst of it was, was the way I felt about it all. I said to myself, *It is all disgusting*. Disgusting: that I thought this really frightened me. I went there feeling sick with love and sorrow at what they might have to do to her;

but when the time came I said it was simply *disgusting*. What happened to me?"

But Marietta said to him not to think that way—he was just so full of worry and horror that all his ideas and feelings were upside down. Sometimes things happened that were too much to bear, and when they did, why, you just made them into something else, in order to bear them.

He didn't know. He could hardly feel. When he thought of his father, his heart turned to ice. He did not dare to think of his mother and when they wheeled her past him to the double doors leading into the operating area he looked away.

There were a few metal armchairs in the bay of the hall-way opposite the operating-room entrance. Max went to lean upon a window looking up a featureless avenue gray in the winter afternoon.

He closed his eyes to the impersonal life of the street below and away. He stood because he could not sit quietly, waiting for the surgeon's report. He nodded his head, saying in the consuming silence, Yes, yes, please, hurry, hurry.

※ ※ ※

"I used to spend hours with her before," said Marietta. She compressed her lips and shook her head against her feeling. She stroked her hair back from her brow and resettled the black ribbon which held it away so that it fell in a dark golden shower to her shoulders. "Alicia was the most of everything I wished I could be," she added.

"How?"

She had to give me a downward smile at my famous word, but she did it fondly, and said,

"Her loveliness, and, what: yes: her *capability*."

We both laughed at the flat moderation of the word, but as Marietta said it, it held more than reckless praise could have. She meant that Aunt Lissy was so clever with her hands—her paintings were really charming, unpretentious, but very skillful, and with an exquisite sense of the damp, fugitive life of flowers. She sewed beautifully, too, and played the piano always at half-voice but with style. She was sensitive to everything that went on in the whole of Chittenden Hills, and without being a busybody, she seemed often to come at just the right moment to be of help to anyone in difficulty. She gave her time and her mind when these could be the best of gifts; and as for the other kind of gift, she was openhanded and unshrewd to the point of provoking the dry protest of her husband who felt that vast wealth imposed an obligation to account for every penny, a business over which she never lingered. She knew that her philanthropies of wealth were at times as useful as those of her spirit, and just as she never measured these, so she never kept a ledger of the others. It was the same when she gave parties. She was like a queen who indicated general wishes, and then with a happy air of surprise and fulfillment enjoyed them when they came true through the imaginative skill of those who served her. The great corridors, rooms, terraces, and vistas of Newstead used to know a magnificence which made even Uncle Alec proud, for the delight of his guests belonged safely to him, as well as to his wife. Her joy was full when her son was old enough to dine with guests, and she saw him through the golden lights and the thronged flowers of her rooms with amusement as dear as her love. He was infinitely charming, he kept up an imposture of diffidence which excused his splendor of face and being, and his mother knew how much of his delightful effectiveness to take credit for, and how much was actually unaccountable. Even then, she had always granted him in her thoughts the freedom to be like nobody but himself, for whom he alone must be responsible. It was a pity he could not draw, but he had every other grace, and she smiled when she thought how his father expected him to become another in the long ancestral chain of Chittendens who actively dealt with the family financial interests first as employees and of course finally in control. Maximilian, she laughingly predicted, would never sit in a paneled office either as a clerk or as an officer. She had no idea what he wanted to do, for neither had he. In the hours when they read aloud to each other, they would pause to talk about his future. His vision of this changed with every year as he grew older, and she followed him asking only that in whatever he did he must think of others as well as himself. With idealism, he promised. Because she was so faithful to him when he needed her in his childhood illnesses, or his disappointments, or his rushes of love for a populous succession of friends, boys and girls, he made his claims on her with confidence. She would never fail him, nor he her, just as neither would ever hurt the other knowingly. He used to laugh at her incessant activity. She kept a secretary busy all day over her appointments and the notes which must precede and follow them. She remained his ideal of the uses of living. She had given him breath, and on his later birthdays he used to write her notes to put under her sitting-room door in which he would thank her for the gift of life. She showed these to Marietta, who was like a daughter to her, and they would say they had never heard of any other son who used his birthday just so. When he did wrong, she did not spare him, but flashed out at him with her wit until he felt ashamed of himself. His childish cruelties were like other children's, but, said Marietta, somehow even at his most wicked he seemed angelic, and his mother had admitted to her that many a time when she was whipping him verbally she could hardly keep from bursting into laughter, and always did so as soon as he had been removed to the nursery to cultivate remorse.

"They were really so like each other, you know, Richard," said Marietta, "without exactly looking alike. It was mostly the way they instantly understood each other about everything. They were quicker than cats at leaping at the same idea. A thousand times I have seen them look at each other when somebody said something, and then start to answer it in exactly the same way, in words, or by laughing out, or, you know, anything. One time he was terribly mean to me and when he came to apologize I refused to answer him. I would *never* forgive him. I was frozen, like a princess whose disfavor means death. He said, 'Oh, look, dear child, save your acting for something worth getting.' It was Alicia's kind of remark, and he even had her amused tone of voice which always put an end to anything pretentious. For a second I was more of a princess than ever, and then the strain was simply too awful and I crumpled, and fell to my knees, and put my hands over my face and laughed. 'That's better,' he said, and simply went home with this work done, with the air of someone with more work to do elsewhere— just like her. As for the apology, it somehow got lost."

I was still young enough to feel much of this within the reference of my own mother and my closeness to her—

though the dimensions were grander here, and we didn't have as much reference to style about our manner of communicating at home. Still, the chaffing love shown by my father, and the sighing gaiety with which my mother gave animation to her duties and concerns, gave me much with which to think of Max and the life he knew and the ordeal which he had come home to.

"He must have thought about all such things," I said, "while he was waiting at the hospital."

Marietta nodded sharply. A glare of lighted coals deep in her eyes made her face look whiter than ever. She had the kind of beauty which proclaims the bone beneath the skin, and raises the image of the skull into mortal loveliness, bringing a pang even while it asks for desire.

※ ※ ※

He must have been waiting for about forty minutes, now standing with his forehead against the cold windowpane—this all took place in ebb-winter—and again tiptoeing to the door to listen, though there was nothing to hear, for two sets of double swinging doors separated him from the operating room. He thought he could hear a remote sound of escaping steam, and there were various antiseptic aromas afloat in the heated air. Now and then an electric bell would make an insistent chiming somewhere far away, and he was reminded of school corridors, where other moments of dread had given him—for reasons long forgotten—a thick, heavy fall of something hollow just where he supposed his stomach would be. Now the fall had turned into something lasting and he wondered if it would ever go away. Suddenly the sound of hissing steam grew briefly louder, and he saw that both sets of double doors had opened and closed allowing the head surgeon to come toward him. The man was all but invisible within his antiseptic wrappings—rumpled, flax-colored muslins, rubber gloves, a mask across his face exposing only deep-lensed, rimless eyeglasses. The doctor's voice was slightly muffled but his remarks were audible. Behind him stood Doctor Osborne, also in operating gown and mask, but subordinate as an observer and family practitioner.

"Max," he said, "this is Doctor de Kranowitz."

"Yes," said the surgeon. "We have the result of the test. It is necessary now to go further. Your mother gave us permission a little while ago, depending on what we found."

It was not really a long hesitation which followed, but long enough for Max to feel as though the weight of the earth were pulling him down. Ever afterward he must behave as though he had no connection with this event. Something enabled him to do so now.

"Do you have to do very much?" he asked.

Doctor de Kranowitz indicated with a finger on his own forearm about where he would make the section.

"We perhaps should take more," he said. "But it is a fairly safe risk to stop here, for we have found this in an early stage."

"Take the risk," said Max impassively. "Save what you can."

"Yes."

"How long will it take?"

"Perhaps two hours."

"Shall I stay? —Yes."

The surgeon nodded and returned at once to the double doors, the escaping steam of the sterilizers, and the task awaiting him. Doctor Osborne said,

"Max."

"Yes?"

"Max," and turned and followed his colleague.

Long later I thought of how it was the living necessity of wounds to heal themselves. When they did, scar tissue was always stronger than the tissue that had been cut or torn. On that day waiting in the hospital Max may have started to heal his inner wound by sealing it off. Perhaps he said to himself out of final necessity that he had not done anything—it was the scarecrow who had done it, and the scarecrow's rake had been thrown down and punished. Otherwise he could not have borne the truth. Let it be forgotten, or if that was not possible, let it be thrust behind legend. He did not consider, just then, the daily reminder in the evidence which his mother could not help exhibiting, however loving her sufferance, and modesty. Did she remember the square dance and the riotous blow? If so, there was never any sign of it. Love knew how to forget as well as remember.

※ ※ ※

"You know?" said Marietta, "lifetimes can happen in two hours. I saw him later that day. It was the day he began to hate. He decided without really knowing it that nobody could ever love him again."

"But hate?"

"Yes. Hate. I told him long afterwards that this was true, and he said it was nonsense. So I never argued. But I saw everything, though we never discussed it, but simply kept on laughing expensively at things to show how really simple and unpretentious we really were."

"I never know just what you mean."

"I know. They all say I talk at right angles."

She gave me a direct, self-deriding smile, and I wished I were one year older than she, instead of two years younger.

"You know what?"

I inquired with a lift of my head, while my eyes pulled at her lips. She said,

"Oh! If we only knew what things keep punishing people inside their heads!" She paused. I waited. She remembered more.

Doctor Osborne brought Max away from the hospital. Presently he said to him in an offhand way,

"Everything was done successfully. De Kranowitz is one of the best. —One thing you must remember, Max," he went on, coming to the heart of his purpose, "is this: there is no certainty of any direct connection between this operation and the incident you told me of, the thing at the barn dance."

He told Marietta later that by the way Max looked at him it was all the boy had been thinking about. "Get it out of your head," added Doctor Osborne roughly, as if scorn would erase another's dangerous thoughts.

Max nodded. They drove up to the Osbornes' house, where Max was to be sheltered that night.

The doctor found his daughter alone for a moment. In a storm of sympathy for Alicia, for her father, for Max, she hugged her father feeling like a child, and rubbed her petal-smooth cheek against his tired, grainy jaw. Hurriedly he told her of the day, and asked if she remembered the Thanksgiving barn dance at Newstead. Yes, she did. Had she seen anything odd that may have happened? She couldn't remember. He told her Max's story about the rake, then said,

"He must not keep thinking about it now. You must help him to forget it if you can. But don't ever, ever mention it to him, because if you do he will think everybody else is thinking about it all the time. Promise, Mari!" She promised. "But if he brings it up himself," said her father, "make him drop the idea."

Oh, she said, nothing she could ever do would make Max do anything. But she would try.

The doctor kissed her troubled forehead and heavily went to ready himself for what must be a bleak dinner.

"And did Max ever mention it?" I asked.

"No," said Marietta.

"Did you?"

"No. —But I almost did several times. —I don't know. He has a secret chamber inside where no one can go. Nobody knows what's in it. I think he doesn't know. If anyone could find it, how happy it might be for us all!"

"Us all?"

"All of us who love him. —Because we do love him, you know."

I remember saying, like a sage, "But I do know. *Somebody* always loves *somebody*."

My manner could have made her shriek with laughter and point at me, but my meaning made her nod with solemnity.

If Aunt Lissy remembered anything about the barn dance, nobody ever knew it, least of all Max; for if he had known that she did, nothing could have kept him from talking with Marietta about it, of this she was sure.

"But didn't your father think the rake thing was really the cause?" I asked.

Marietta put her hands to her mouth as if to pray silence. In the dappled shade from the great oak tree by the creek, she shook her head, saying silently, like the child who is fearful of breaking a spell, *Never ask that!*

The memory of that evening after the operation was again strongly alive for her. She seemed to want me to know all she could tell me, however painful for her to revive it.

"When they came to tell him it was over, do you know what he thought of? He told me that night, back at home, I mean at my house, where my father brought him."

They tried to make a meal at dinner, but managed poorly at it. Later, the Osborne parents left Marietta and Maximilian alone. They huddled in the dark in front of a library wood fire. They let the fire go out. Max said little at first, and that was spaced out until the ashes were cold. They lay locked in each other's arms on the hearth rug, passionless, united, hungry, and somber in thought. Pressing no claims on each other, they implicitly gave each other the ultimate claim, and thereafter took it for granted that they were given to each other, and one day would prove it in the flesh. She thought he slept at moments, but just when his breathing seemed to go easy and mindless, he would say something, and she shivered at holding in her arms the nursery king whom she had tried to burn to death, the cruel playmate who owed her a thousand apologies and had never given one, and she heard him as clearly as though he had not said a word. She read in her mind a coherent recital which she made of his private allusions and long silent gaps between them, rather as though she were deciphering a poem of the post World War I style.

There was, at the end of the work in the surgery, a quick current of activity—doors swinging, persons departing for other rooms, others entering to clean the premises, orderlies taking orders, nurses processing alongside doctors, and rubber-tired wheels bearing away an inert figure classically folded in sweeps of white cloth. Max waited but no one came for him for a long time. He had no idea of where to go. He looked out the cold window. Evening and snow were falling together. Electric vistas in the hushed streets were now indescribably lovely. He saw them even as he thought of something else.

One time when he was a small child, running and playing out of doors, one of his shoelaces came untied. He trod on it and fell and bumped his head on the edge of the flagstone terrace on the south side of Newstead. His mother was sitting in a pool of light and shade under a great maple tree. She was working at needlepoint. She put down her frame and went rapidly but without excitement to him, took him up, kissed the hot lump that was rising on his wide, clear forehead to make it well, and hushed him with her concern, though surely he would have liked her to show a little more indignation at his unjust fate. She took him to her tree and murmuring coolly to him, held him on her lap and took up his small inert foot and addressed a droll scolding to the wicked shoelace which had brought on the mishap. She then tied the lace in good, tight loops, and he remembered his staring fascination at how she did it—the flashing cleverness of her hands, the shuttling skill of her lovely, capable fingers at their little task. Who else ever tied a shoelace with that swift neatness, and made such pleasant sounds so close to the ear that he could feel cool lips on his hot, outraged cheeks? Thick-handed nursemaids until then. How quickly all was mended now.

If memory would only mend as firmly at it revived. Doctor Osborne finally came to take him home. There was nothing more to do here. Maximilian had done all he was supposed to do; and it was more than he knew how to do. He could not remember whether his mother had ever finished that piece of needlepoint that day under the tree by the terrace.

In the meadow, in the long grass dappled by the old oak, alongside the pale little brook, I presently said,

"I wonder when I will see Max's mother."

"Today. We are all lunching together," said Marietta, "at Newstead."

"Are you coming too?"

"Yes."

"I am glad."

"I may help."

"Help?"

"Oh—to dilute it all by one more part."

"Everything is so still in the huge house," I said.

"The house has never recovered."

I heard how Alicia, my Cousin Lissy, my Aunt Lissy, slowly won her way back to a sense of life. It took years. The general commiseration was hardest to bear of all her trials, and she wondered when she might ever confront people at large again. She thought of going abroad, which the doctors approved; but one day she told Doctor Osborne that if she went, she might never return, for her victory would have to

be won here, at home, in the most painfully familiar surroundings, or it might never be won at all. Merriman
Osborne, after a moment's reflection, agreed with her. She
was determined to stare down her difficulties every day
without the aid of fleeting distractions. If she ran away from
them, and later returned, perhaps in high spirits, and met
them again, her whole life might collapse as her husband's
had done. His illness was one of her great trials. The other
was a stony change in her son's feeling for her—in his very
behavior as he struggled to leave adolescence and enter early
manhood. Neither of these burdens ever entered into her
conversation with even intimate friends. But they saw how
the weight of both held back her own recovery, and cost her
the serene beauty of her own countenance. They had always
said that she never seemed aware of her beauty—until it was
gone. Not that she spoke of it; but a veil of delicate shame
seemed to hang before her face. When people told her, now,
how lovely she was, she knew they were saying it to conceal
the opposite from her—as if they could. I would soon see for
myself how all this was.

As for Uncle Alec, his nervous prostration kept him upstairs for a year. Having failed, at love and duty, he col-
lapsed; and then, having to admit his failure, the knowledge
of it extended his state of shock. He was another year in
getting back to his office for an hour or two each day. Everyone said that it was Lord Byron who saved him. Doctor
Osborne dated the beginning of his slow recovery, which
would never actually be complete, from the time when
Uncle Alec thought of his father's genteel hobby and decided to make it the best private collection in the world on
the subject. He resigned as chairman of the Chittenden
board, reverting to the position of a simple member, who

now voted, where previously he had disposed. His active life had been built upon a talent for abstractions—the upper configurations of finance. Now he gave himself to another —the itemization of a life once prodigal in its hot lusts, but now merely subject to record.

Between these two maimed parents, my Cousin Max grew from schoolboy into college man with an air of solicitous affability which served for the most part to conceal another impulse entirely—a desire to find feeling in himself by whatever means.

❧ ❧ ❧

"Come on," said Max at two minutes before one o'clock, leaning into my room. "We must be punctual. I hate it, but in the end it is simpler."

I was ready. We went along the second-floor corridor to the great central court where the stairway divided above the high door to the drawing room. As we came to the stairs, a door opened beyond, and in a blur of reflected light, Maximilian's mother came into the hall. We halted as she approached.

"Mummy, this is Richard," said Max. He pointed a finger at me as if I were a comic specimen whom he had never seen before. He was suddenly constrained.

"My dear Richard": said Mrs Chittenden. She held her left hand to me. She wore pale gray silk gloves on both hands. Habitually, she supported the right with the left, for it seemed heavy and immovable, a carved, useless representation of a hand with fingers delicately, and permanently, arched.

[69]

"My dear cousin's boy. How like her you are." I had always thought I resembled my father. She turned to Max. "Shall we go down?" He nodded, expecting his duty. He came to her left side. She took his arm and slowly we descended the marble stairs which were made comfortable by a lane of dark crimson velvet. I followed by a step or two. Waiting below were Uncle Alec and Marietta.

"Good morning, Lissy, my dear," said Uncle Alec with his laryngeal scratch. He smiled at her sideways. She nodded pleasantly at him, and spoke to Marietta, who replied,

"Aunt Lissy, may I come this way?"—indicating her riding clothes. A kind smile was her answer and we proceeded through the great drawing room to the rotunda of marble columns and glass, with trellises of greens, where luncheon was set at a small round glass table. Max ceremonially seated his mother. Uncle Alec took a chair facing her. I was at her right, between them. Max and Marietta were opposite me. From behind a tall screen of many folds painted to show an Italian landscape, two serving maids in black with white caps, aprons and gloves, immediately began to serve lunch. As Aunt Lissy turned to take a morsel I was able to gaze at her forgetful of being watched.

※ ※ ※

She was like a season's end, with a premonition of further change to come, and in her, beauty was the season. She was my mother's age, I knew, and yet I could not keep her there, for she seemed a generation older. I thought she looked like a ghost that yet waited to go. She gave an effect of silver pointed up with touches of black. Her eyes were black, surrounded by lashes so thick and black they made me think—without prejudice—of spiders' legs. Her brows were also dark, and when she chose, she could make her eyes sparkle, or seem to, by deliberately contracting all the blacks and smiling, so that light was trapped for an instant before it was reflected in a flash. Not quite a double blink, it must have been a facial gesture developed for the reassurance of others during her long convalescence, when it would have been a great effort to say much or move bodily. Her face was narrow and surprisingly smooth, but age, too soon, pressed its contours downward. She was always heavily powdered and wore no other cosmetic. In her upper lip a few small wrinkles converged toward the center like those of rueful monkeys I had seen in the zoo, and the faintest fur was made visible there by the powder that lodged in it and in the convergent lines. Her lips were unrouged. Their outline was blurred, as though eroded by years of compression toward a center of denied expression of violent or anguished feeling. She wore much the same costume every daytime that I saw her—a plain dress of fine gray or pale blue or champagne-colored silk, with high collar, full sleeves, and skirts so long that they caught in carpets. When she moved it was with composed grace, and when she spoke her voice was cool, clear, and faint, as if distantly overheard. Always she held her fixed, artificial right hand and forearm with her live left hand, both always gloved alike. Her hair was silvery, done in dove wings that swept past her ears, showing them and the earrings of small, single, gray pearls which she always wore. A fine veil of black threads held her hair in place and came down over her brow and eyes and added a degree of shadowed charm to her glance. When she made her eyes sparkle, the veil was like delicate foliage behind which lights moved briefly.

"Tell her," my mother had said, "that I always try to imitate her expression when I want someone to give me something. Tell her I never do it properly. There was nobody else at school whom we all tried to be like. Ask her if she remembers the picnic at Lilydale, and how dreadfully I behaved. Tell her she must forgive me even now. Tell her."

But Aunt Lissy was one of those who outlive their shared moments of the past, which the others of the time never forget, but tug at her in their memories, as if she might save for them what was already gone.

❀ ❀ ❀

The laws of occasion ruled at Newstead when people gathered. True to breeding and class, my cousins—except for Maximilian—enacted the proper imposture of mutual interest and response. When one spoke, another half-smiling, as if in marveling regard across the table, gave visible and, at suitable moments, audible support. Uncle Alec made the first play. Turning his pale head aside, and lifting his pinched profile with its curving nose so that he seemed to take energy from the air through his long, thin nostrils, he said with muted waggery,

"Lissy, I think we have another recruit for the growing aamy of Lord Byron's loyal followers. Our visiting cousin positively devoured me all morning in the libr'y. —D'you know my word for it, Richard?"

Aunt Lissy forced her furry twinkle at me to share her husband's wit with me in advance, and when it came, she gave her eyes to him to tell everyone how clever he was.

"I mean," he continued, "what my father called a *hobby,* I always call *h-obsession.*"

As Max's spirits visibly fell at this statement, Marietta loyally showed animation. She put her hands on Uncle Alec's near arm and let him feel her inner temblor for a moment. "Oh, Alexander Chittenden—" she said, and stopped, as if choked with admiration. I laughed dutifully. He bowed slightly.

"How delicious, Alec," said his wife, as if she had not heard his pun a hundred times. I knew later that they never exchanged a word except in company.

"People have probably told you you ought to send that in," said Marietta. "I adore it when they say things like that. Send it in *where?* Where is *in?*"

"Oh: oh: the *Sat'day Evening Post,* of course," said Uncle Alec. "Wherever else?"

"We are all loyal Philadelphians," murmured Max.

"Ceetainly, my dear," said his father, making affirmative the disagreeable cast of Max's remark. Max was not to be sold out so cheaply.

"Will that take care of Lord Byron for the moment?" he asked, with a spectacular smile of false innocence which made Marietta see him with a starved look.

"No, I have a question," said his mother, to protect her husband from his son's unkindness.

"Oh, bully," cried Uncle Alec.

"What did you find in Mr Dana's catalogues this morning?"

"You knew? That he brought some? How on eeth?"

Mr Dana always brought some, so the question was a safe one, but Aunt Lissy chose to give a mysterious little shrug as if to say she had her ways of knowing.

"Well, actually," continued Uncle Alec, "there *is* an item sure to turn up at Sotheby's if we don't get there feest. A quite wonderful one. A copy of Lady Blessington with marginalia in Moore's handwriting."

"Oh, Alec. Surely you have already—"

"We cabled before lunch."

"Oh, how splendid."

And now, with Byron carried far enough to obliterate Max's rudeness, Aunt Lissy was ready to drop him in her turn. She turned to me and found me staring at her false hand as it rested on her closed left hand. I looked away before I could look at her face, and when I did, I found her eyes waiting for mine in the kindest forgiveness. She blinked them both, as if to say that many people of greater experience than mine had been unable to ignore the fascination of her visible disadvantage, and that she had long grown used to being an object of natural curiosity. As I read something like this into her smile, I blushed deeply.

"Mummy," said Max, inexorably, "stop punishing Richard. You've made him blush for something he couldn't help."

She did not turn away from me to him and so I saw the pain that came and went swiftly in her face. She said to me,

"Well, you may as well know it, Richard, I have my own h-obsession, also."

Uncle Alec swayed in his chair with pleasure at the quotation.

"Do tell us, Lissy," he said, unnecessarily, with a birdlike turn of his narrow head.

"Well, you know, Richard, once upon a time, a long time ago, I used to amuse myself and burden my friends by painting flowers and giving them away. Now I've gone one step farther. I have become a horticulturist."

"Max showed me the great greenhouse," I said. "It looks like the botanical gardens at home in Dorchester."

"Max called it the Crystal Palace when we built it. He saw a picture in an old *Illustrated London News* in the library which made him think of it. —Darling," she said, turning to him, "would you be a lamb and drive me down there after lunch? There is something wonderfully exciting going on. Mr Standish telephoned me this morning about it. —Mr Standish is our head gardener," she explained to me. She waited, facing me, fearful of what Max would say.

"If you like," he said, "though perhaps Frazier or somebody could follow in another car and let me go on from there."

He meant that with three chauffeurs and a dozen motorcars available, it did seem regrettable that she should make him drive her the two and a quarter miles to the greenhouse when he might well have other things to do with his afternoon.

"We'll take Richard and Marietta with us," said his mother, "I really am quite excited about what is happening."

"Oh, what: what, Lissy," demanded Uncle Alec with dim animation.

"My night-blooming cereus," she said. "Mr Standish says it will surely open either tonight or tomorrow night. He has been watching it night and day."

"D'you mean," asked Uncle Alec for my benefit, so that I would be properly instructed in the nature of the marvel, "that it blooms only in the nighttime?"

"Yes," said Max before his mother could answer, "as its name implies, or rather, affirms."

"It is the only one in this whole part of the country," said Aunt Lissy. "Unimaginably lovely. This one has never opened before. We must all watch it."

Her eagerness was depressing, for no one else really shared it. She turned to her son.

"I know," she said.

"You know what, Mummy?"

"About you and flowers."

"I do have other interests."

"Yes, but flowers bore you. —My flowers, mostly, I suppose," and she made a slow, coquettish smile for him, which sought to grant him the freedom he had already seized. "Never mind. We won't be long—I just want to run down and see it at this stage, and of course we cannot expect anything to happen by day."

"Oh, no, never, never," exclaimed Marietta nervously. She wanted to turn on Max and claw him for his unkindness and then kiss him. Aunt Lissy caught this and said,

"Please: Mari darling: let him alone. He has learned at Harvard that one must not love one's mother." She gave Max another pulling smile, to suggest to the world that their devotion was secure under all this rude banter. He shrugged away her invisible reach. He knew how by many small claims upon him—a drive to the Crystal Palace and back—she tried to recover the large central claim that was gone. She turned to me. "You will still be here?"

"I believe he leaves day after tomorrow," said Uncle Alec.

"We must have it for you."

"I hope so," I said, "I have never seen one."

"I do so hope it will open while you are here," she said.

She dared to show her real excitement over the night-blooming cereus when she talked to me about it, and I am sure my face took on the look of open wonder that showed on hers. Her animation seemed almost to exhaust her even as it gave off light and heat.

"All this commotion," said Max, "over a stage in the life cycle of a vegetable obscenity. Really."

"Max, really," murmured his father.

"Oh, is it? Is it?" asked Marietta with relief to have a real scandal to turn to.

"I am sure no one knows what he means," said Aunt Lissy.

"I know precisely. The typical stalk of the affair is unmistakably phallic. That it will be crowned by some sort of emitted blossom is merely a flourish of metaphor."

Aunt Lissy was equal to the attack. She leaned forward, cradling her lost hand, and said with velvety control,

"But how fascinating, dear. One would never have thought of it in that way, but any dimension of reference is of interest, and an occasional one is astonishing. I find your remark astonishing."

"It was meant to be," he said, and smiled upon his mother with his brows drawn together, so that the resemblance between mother and son was striking for a moment. She closed her mouth so firmly over what she was tempted to say next that a tiny fall of powder left her upper lip. If her son was young, articulate, and reckless, he would find his mother restrained in her answer to him while she lived. The strength of suffering and loss, futility acknowledged, and unpierced solitude belonged to her. I gave her a secret look, hunting for the girl within her whom my mother remembered with such long devotion. I saw nothing but the care-laden presence of a semi-invalid who, as everyone knew, tired easily, but bravely.

Yet how could anyone's fortitude be so crushing? Because —the knowledge is now mine—it was fashioned of the very reasons which always ask too much of love.

Our silence lasted too long for Uncle Alec.

"Lissy," he called like a proud husband, "tell us about your plans for this evening!"

"Everything is done. We finished the seating this morning. Miss Magruder is leaving a copy of the diagram on your desk."

"Are we to have music?"

"Oh, yes."

"And the young things will dance. —What time do we have the fireworks concert?"

"At half-past ten, between supper and the dancing."

"You mustn't do too much this afternoon, Lissy," he said, suddenly reviving his executive manner, "we want you to sparkle tonight. Hang every bauble from your jewel box on yourself wherever you can."

"Oh," she cried, "not for a fireworks party, do you think?"

For some reason this set Marietta to laughing. Aunt Lissy was grateful. She caught the contagion of relief in Marietta's laughter, and began to laugh with her, until great lateral tears appeared between her thick lashes and swam with light. The muscular effort of the laugh brought a spasm of some sort to her right arm and she lifted it and lowered it to ease pain. Laughing, she wore the look of someone weeping. How could I ever remember all this to tell at home?

"Lissy, may we have coffee in the lib'ry?" —Uncle Alec clearly felt it was time to adjourn such a luncheon party. She

[78]

nodded and readied to rise. I sprang to pull her chair for her.

"Thank you, Richard," she said fondly, and while Maximilian glared, she took my arm and walked with me to the library, where a manservant was just entering with a coffee tray.

"Yes. Peefectly. Yes," mused Uncle Alec, as he saw his household functioning well.

❦ ❦ ❦

Half an hour later we stood—Aunt Lissy, Max, Marietta, and myself—in a far aisle of the Crystal Palace listening to Mr Standish make his report. He spoke slowly in a smoky voice and with the emphasis of someone who knew and loved his job.

"I have kept it in normal conditions," he said, "without forcing in any way. Just the natural light and temperature of this wing of the house. I noticed the buds changing color four days ago—"

"Growing paler?" asked Aunt Lissy.

"Yes, ma'am, and somewhat waxy-looking, though nothing t'what they'll be later when open."

"You have seen a cereus in bloom elsewhere?"

"Yes, ma'am. —And then I checked about every hour to see the rate of change; and I am confi-dent that we can't be kept waiting much more than twenty-four hours."

"Whatever shall we do if it should decide to open to-night!" she exclaimed. Mr Standish, ruddy, stocky, and even-minded, remained silent but his question was visible on his face. "I mean," she added, "we are having this unnerving party in the greenhouse tonight and out on the terrace, and I wouldn't want not to be able to come and stay with the flower when it begins. —You *will* notify me, Mr Standish? Wherever and whenever?"

"Oh, yes, ma'am. I don't guarantee, for when they start they sometimes move fast—"

"One can actually see the petals unfold?" asked Marietta.

"Yes, ma'am." He pursed the stubby fingers of his right hand to make a closed bud, and then opened them very slowly. "You can see it happen as easy as this. Slower, but moving."

Aunt Lissy looked at me with radiance.

"Richard, isn't it going to be wonderful?"

On the waist-high bench holding carefully raked damp earth the night-blooming cereus stood alone. It was in a wooden tub which rested on a square flagstone. The plant had five thick dark green stalks, each reaching generally upward in a different radius. Each was finely defended by a mist of pale needles. A closed bud stood on a short stem at the tip of each stalk. We had heard so much of the living movement of the flowers that they now seemed to be sleeping, and we stood waiting to be told when they would awaken. Beyond the plant which was the object of so much energy, planning, care, and expense, receded the perspective of the Crystal Palace in moist air that grew bluer the farther the eye reached within the glass walls. Mr Standish kept his candid countryman's gaze upon his ma'am. His concern for the plant was as real as hers, but perhaps his had an even closer intimacy with it, for he was responsible in a way she did not share. He was the guardian; she merely the owner.

"Oh—how intense!" exclaimed Marietta, somehow enacting the word itself in her posture. She looked at Max for approval, but he maintained his calm.

"Yes," said Aunt Lissy with a hint of apology and sadness, "I suppose it is. And yet, why not?" She turned to me and the longing in her face brought a remote thump to my breast. She seemed to say that if I might think she was merely displaying a pleasing interest in an expensive plaything, I was wrong. It must be clear that here was her earnest and loving absorption—the life of this flower to which she gave time and thought. What else in life just now was there to demand her interest? to help her forget pain? to keep her from going mad? to hold her from dying? Look around me, she implored silently, and say who makes claim upon my existence? For the love of God, believe in my flowers with me, and don't nod kindly at a whimsical preoccupation which helps to fill my days. My excitement is real. Let it remain so. Help me. Exclaim in wonder at the marvel I offer you—all I have to offer.

❦ ❦ ❦

Was I confronting another of those barriers, as I called them earlier, or perhaps I could call them tests, by the passing of which we mark stages of growth? I remember the way my parents, trying to conceal their vigilance but failing, would watch how I met my encounters with new experience and knowledge. They knew in that summer how I was coming to the stage of life when I would begin to see the lives of other families in relation to my own, and they could only wonder how I would judge not only the new, but the old. They had pressed me to come to Newstead, and they surely waited to discover what I would bring home. I don't know how explicitly I told them later, but they must have seen that for the first time I was aware of the possibility that the lives all about us consisted of two aspects—the outer one shown to the world and maintained as long as dignity or desperation made this possible; and the inner one which in the end could never be wholly concealed. There was much pathos in the realization that it was just the most imperatively kept secrets which in the end revealed themselves through the mere being of their possessors. In my country the rich could never be wrong about anything—so we grew up believing. Could we blame them for fostering this convention themselves? Looking homeward from the Crystal Palace I was suffused by a wave of homesickness; for I longed to be at ease in the Chittenden Hills, but the Chittendens, in their various self-centered needs, made this impossible.

"Marietta," I thought, realizing that when I was away from her, I felt unlike myself. I now sought refuge in her. For the first time I was in love for more than a few hours.

※ ※ ※

She left us at the hilltop when we brought Aunt Lissy back from the greenhouse.

"Dance with me this evening," she said, as we saw her mounted and ready to ride home. "Both of you."

Max nodded abruptly and she gathered her mount and rode away.

"Come with me, now," said Max.

"What are we going to do?"

"We'll drive down to Standish's house and pick up my dog and exercise him for a while."

"I must be back at four. Your mother is expecting me for a little talk and some tea after her rest."

"We'll be back. Let's remember something."

"What."

"When we're as old as they are, let's remember how it is to be as young as we are now."

"Don't they remember?"

He shrugged hopelessly. His disarming charm settled over him again. When he was unsure of himself, he was at his best, though I envied what I thought of as his sophistication.

"You know? Richie? I really don't know. I have thought about this problem a lot. It is really quite a problem. Once or twice I have thought that the trouble is that they remember too well how it was to be young and sure of everything; and that what makes them the way they are now is that they can't bear to think of everything they have learned since. I don't know. The more everything seems less certain, the more they have to act as though it were more so."

I frowned to conceal my determination to talk that way. Would I ever go to Harvard? We changed cars, leaving the sumptuous old Packard, which looked like a galleon with its high poop, in which we had ridden down to the Crystal Palace earlier, and vaulted into the Isotta. It was well dried out since the night before. Max laughed as we drove off in a roar like a battery salute.

"Frazier told me I would do well not to leave empty whiskey bottles in my car."

"Perhaps you wanted the bottle to be seen."

He turned to face me with delighted amazement.

"Richie, that's the line! Get behind what anything says to what it might mean. It doesn't matter if you turn out to be wrong. The thing is, to shake 'em up with what you say."

Perhaps I was learning how to talk that way right now.

"Why does your dog live at Mr Standish's?"

He made a great slash at the air with his hand and said that it was all right for him to have a dog in his *rooms,* but the trouble was, to go there, it would have to go through the rest of the house, and this would create disorder, they believed, and so it had been arranged, without his taking part in the discussion, for Chief, his dog, who was a fire-house dog, or Dalmatian, to live two and a quarter miles down the road with the head gardener's family, who would take the best of care of him.

"I have visiting privileges," said Max wryly. "When I can, I go down there and take him out for a run. He loves to run alongside the road and keep up with me as I drive along. He's the most stupid animal I ever saw, and this makes you love him, you see?"

He said that he had thought a couple of years ago that he might work out a rig to bring Chief up to his window with a basket and a rope, and they had tried it out.

"Chief would get in the basket and sit down, and Frazier would back off a little holding the coil of rope one end of which was attached to the handle. Every time he began to throw the rope up to me at the window, Chief would jump out and chase the rope. When he caught it, he shook it and gruffled over it, looking up at me with one eye—he has one green and one brown eye—to see how pleased I was. We tried tying him in the basket but he thrashed about so that he always tipped the basket over and ruined the balance. We never got it to work."

We went roller-coasting along the narrow gray road, swooping with the little hills. Soon we saw the greenhouse and just beyond it the gardener's house, which I had not noticed before. The road ran on past and was lost in a high ridge. How could it be that one of the richest boys in the nation could not keep a dog with him? Max said,

"What would you do, if you were I?"

"If I were twenty-one I would say politely but firmly as I was now of age that I would have my dog with me or I would have to live somewhere else."

"Oh, no, no, I don't mean about the dog. I mean about everything."

I had not thought about "everything"—I was too full of impressions, some bewildering, some beguiling, to have an answer. Out of my confusion leaped a question in return.

"Why do you behave like that to your mother?"

His profile, with its regularly spaced notches clear against the sky, grew still and severe.

"It is a pity you didn't know her before, as she used to be," he replied coldly. It was all the answer he was going to make. Anyhow, we were drawing up to the gardener's white cottage. Waiting at the gate in the low white picket fence was the Dalmatian, who knew the sound of the Isotta. Max skidded the tires to a halt and leaped out. The tall dog, with its bright black marks in its smooth white coat, leaped up to greet him, and they clasped each other at the neck and made two or three turns in a hilarious waltz. Chief barked and Max imitated him. They both threw their heads back and bayed. Then they danced apart and Max, waving me to come along, ran down the road to a rail fence at the edge of a meadow and sailed over it. Chief followed, and then I. We played Chase the Stick, with Chief cantering between us to retrieve as we threw a stick back and forth. Sometimes we let him get it, and then we had to play hunter and prey, stalking the dog who would let us approach almost within reach before he heaved himself up to plunge farther away in the tall, pungent grass. Max gave a brilliant performance pretending to be a coach dog like Chief, and Chief, in the spirit of the game, honored the impersonation. Soon we were exhausted not from exercise but from laughter and we all three came to ground in the middle of the meadow panting and looking at the sky.

"By God, it's hot," said Max.

"Yes. Awfully."

"It's great, isn't it!"

"No. I hate it."

"Oh, no, summer is the best time."

"Yes. I believe you are a summer man."

"Is that good?"

He could never forego occasion for praise, the garland of forgiveness. He courted it mockingly, yet with a hint of pleading.

"Well, it's good for you, I suppose. It wouldn't be for me."

The answer was not satisfactory. He desired to be what everyone else could hope to be.

"Richie, God damn it, I don't know what to make of you. Sometimes I think I've got you pinned down to the mat, and then you pull a surprise maneuver, and off you go."

"Why do you care what I think?"

"I guess it is because you won't really tell me. I have to find out."

I replied to this with silence and a steady gaze. His spirits fell. He said,

"I wish I knew what was the matter with me."

Now it was my turn to seek. I had not thought about what might be the matter with him, if anything really was, which I could not believe for I did not know what to do with knowledge.

"Is something wrong, Max?"

He rolled over in the tall grass and put his face down into the cradle of his arms.

"I think just about everything," he answered in a voice muffled against the soft damp secret earth.

I waited. I had no experience out of which to make the next inquiry which would enlighten me or deliver him. Chief lay nearby, panting sociably. With his tongue hanging out and his teeth shining, he looked like a lost guest smiling at a party.

Presently Max said,

"When I'm away, I remember how badly I acted at home, and I swear when I am home the next time I will show them all that I love them. I will make them forget how offensive I have been, and I tell myself that I need not say much of anything, but only let them feel that I love them and am grateful for everything they have given me." He rolled to his side and faced me. "Do you feel that for your own family? *when you're with them?*"

"Yes."

"Then why don't I? —After I make my promises to myself that I will be the son they want, I always feel good for days. I write home and jabber about everything and anything. I think of things to make them laugh, as they read my letters. I sleep better for weeks. I even do a little work—I mean, more than just the necessary. And then."

I nodded.

"And then," he continued, "I come home, and when I see them again, and how everything is, it all starts again. I hurt them twenty times a day, I see myself doing it, I get disgusted with myself, and that makes me act all the worse toward them. They can't even take notice any more. My mother told me she had decided never to shed tears again, over me, or anything. Marietta is the only hope, and I treat her like hell sometimes."

"She's great."

"Yes, I know. She thinks you are, too. She and my mother have had a long talk about you. They think you're good for me. They wish I were like you."

I laughed. If he only knew how I longed to be a Max, handsome, brilliant, careless, cruel yet irresistible, a prince who lived in disguise most of the time.

He jumped up. Come, he motioned. He gave Chief a whack on his glossy hard rump, and we all ran to the car and were off down the road toward the curtain of hills ahead. We passed a boarded-up schoolhouse. We saw cows in one field and horses in another. The road crossed a little brook. We flew over it. Faintly through the wind of our speed I thought I heard a train whistle and looked at Max. A train seemed a most unlikely thing to find in those pastoral hills. He nodded and pointed. Along the floor of the valley close to the ridge ahead ran a track. I saw a small black engine trolling toward us under a skein of white smoke. It pulled four freight cars. Soon we could see the crossing. Max calculated the closing angle of our speed and the train's. For a quarter of a mile he navigated nicely as the collision course he was dramatizing became more and more certain in its elements of distance, nearness, speed, time, and power. I began to feel the excited joyful horror which I always knew watching a black and white movie comedy, when the train and the Ford car full of cops ran toward each other. Max gave a shout and pressed the gas pedal. The trainmen saw us now, and began tooting violently on their three-note chord of steam and flue. Max waved to show that he saw them. They rolled the engine bell and we could hear the hot scream of iron brakes. The road lifted, it took us up to the crossing, we bumped hard on the rails, and I half stood up staring at the engine which grew and grew in my vision until everything looked black, except the engineer's eyes, which were bright blue, and his red face, which was ready to burst with fury. He opened his mouth to shout and so close were we in that closing instant that I saw a gold tooth in the flash of afternoon. With one inch and a half-second to spare we were across and as the engine rang heavily past us we could feel its wind on our necks. The engineer released his brakes and the little train took a curve at the base of the hills. The fireman was leaning out of his cab window shaking his fist at us. Max let the car coast down to an ambling speed. He was laughing and shouting.

"Next time I won't give him so much leeway!"

"You damned near got us knocked off," I said. "You God damned fool!"

"Wasn't it great?"

"I'm not so sure. —I admit it was exciting."

"He'll report me. Nobody's supposed to play with a railroad."

"Where does it go?"

"It's a little junction line. Once every morning a passenger train comes down to Olympia, and goes back up in the late afternoon. And once every afternoon that freight train goes up, and comes down between ten and eleven o'clock at night. They used to let me ride in the engine when I was young."

When he was young. As soon as he said this, I realized how old he had seemed to me. Childhood should not end suddenly, as his had ended. I think now of Byron, and the uses of scorn to cauterize early wounds.

"Where does this road go?" I asked.

"Only to the quarry." He pointed to the rise before us. The road wound out of sight in a fold of the hills. As we left the flat valley we saw a small brick house contained against the meadows by a tall hedge of laurel.

"Who is there?"

"That is where the Danas live—he is my father's librarian. You met him."

"Oh yes."

"It is a nice house. I always wanted it for myself. Maybe some day I will have it. It is the only house across the railroad tracks. There would be nobody to keep track of my coming and goings."

We drove toward the barrier of the ridge, but Max let the car slacken its speed with the effect of revealing a pause in his thought. Suddenly he asked,

"Do you like children?"

"I suppose so—like everybody."

"No, but *do you feel their lives?* They are the greatest. They cannot lie. When a child tries to lie, even the artifice of it is an honest betrayal. You know the great secret?"

"I—probably not."

"It is to keep alive the child inside, alongside the man growing up."

"I thought we were supposed to outgrow various stages of life."

"Nonsense. We must keep every one as we enter the next. —Let's go to see my children."

Before I could ask who and where they were, he was turning around and heading back toward the Dana cottage. Drawing up parallel to the laurel hedge he stopped the car and leaped out, calling to me to follow. In the rear of the house he found a gateway through the hedge, and within, he found the two children of the Dana family. They were a boy four years old and a girl two. On seeing Max, they lost their heads. They screamed for him, "Uncle Max, Uncle Max," and began running in circles like ponies in a ring, showing off in delight, their heads down, the girl imitating her brother, their hard little chests pumping. Max chased them, caught them, and took one up in each arm. They kicked and strove for freedom hoping he would not let them go. His face shone with pleasure; perhaps even with love. All at once after this initial show of energy they settled down and I was introduced as "Cousin Richard whom you must love very much," and a dialogue followed in mock gravity, during which Max gave an exhibition of how to use the child within him as he sought the children without.

He asked for their news. They had none until he particularized for them.

"How is the cat?"

"Fine."

"Where is she?"

"She is there."

"Where?"

"I don't know."

"Is she off in the field looking for fieldmice?"

"Yes."

"Will she find any?"

"I don't know."

"Do you love fieldmice?"

"Yes."

"Do we want the kitty to let them go?"

"No."

"Yes."

"Yes."

"How is the goldfish in the house?"

"Fine."

"Does he swim all day long?"

"Yes."

"Would the kitty get him if he isn't careful?"

"No."

"Yes."

"Yes."

"We don't want the kitty to get the goldfish, do we?"

"No."

"That's right. What does the goldfish say?"

"Nothing."

"Oh yes he does—he says *gwup-gwup-gwup*. Doesn't he?"

"Yes."

"Say it."

"Wup-wup-wup."

"Ve-ry good. How are the spiders in the garden?"

"Fine. —We have one."

"You do? Have you seen him?"

"Yes."

"Can you show him to me?"

"Yes."

"Where is he?"

"There."

"Show me."

They made a small procession, going to an old rickety arbor where, sure enough, spun as if by the heat-veiled summer sunlight, a misty web was spread between the upright and a diagonal support of the arbor under an overhang of limp vine leaves. In its center was a great brown spider hung in wary stillness. In a whisper which was used to promote danger and mystery, Max said,

"If we leave him alone he will not bite."

"Not bite."

But the idea stirred the little girl. She reached for the protection of Max's arms. He hoisted her aloft to face him. She was serious. She brought her great eyes close to his and put her finger on his mouth and watched her finger and his lips and then took her finger away and with a blow of breath threw her thick little arms around his neck and kissed him passionately. At this, her brother felt the need of attention. He grasped Max about the thigh and threw his head back and hanging heavily away swung his body, so like that of a *putto,* from side to side, making a high song within his closed lips. Soon enough it was time to let go, but they would not let go. Max had to put them off and set them down on the grass. It was question time again.

"How is the little celluloid boat I brought you last time?"

"Fine."

"Do you play with it in the bath?"

"Yes."

"Do you bathe together in the tub?"

"Yes."

I felt a stir of something alien.

"Do Mummy and Daddy bathe together in the tub?"

"Yes."

"Does the kitty bathe with everybody in the tub?"

"Yes."

"*No.*"

"No."

"The kitty does not like to get wet. Now tell me—"

The mother appeared at the back door and stood inside the screen. She greeted Max and he waved, laughing, comfortable in his privileges, which included ownership of employee family secrets granted by small children. She was heavily pregnant. Her straight dark hair hung in limp hanks beside her tinted glasses which gave her owl eyes. She was so uncomfortable and unattractive in her weighted condition that she thrust it proudly at us with every air of challenge in her knowledge of herself as a woman mindlessly at the mercy of woman's utmost function. I was introduced.

"Jane, this is my Cousin Richard. He's visiting. He's already met Andy at the house."

"Hel-laow," said Mrs Dana.

"We've been having a romp," said Max.

"Yes, I knaow. I could hear in the kitchen."

Max laughed.

"Good-by, chickadees," he shouted to the children, who dragged at him and hung on him all the way to the gate. He kissed them and we left.

Resuming the road toward the ridge, he said,

"Why do they love me?"

"Because you love them and want them to love you."

"No, no. It's more than that. —They know exactly how beautiful they are and how they are made of nothing else, as yet, but love itself. It is not that they are morally pure—actually they will commit tiny crimes to achieve what they want which is love—it is that they are love in the flesh, in its unadulterated state. When I get depressed I remember that they, anyhow, will always scream and jump for me if I go to them. They will not ask me any questions which their lovely little bodies cannot answer for themselves. *My* internal child wants to be as direct and as pure as that."

"Can it?"

"How can it? Never. It is too late." He stared at the hill face of the ridge, which we were rapidly approaching, and added, "How lucky are those who never know ahead of time that everything is *always* too late."

"Why did you ask them about the parents taking baths together? Was that necessary?"

"Necessary?" He laughed. "Necessity doesn't come into it. It was an amusing notion that just came to me. It wouldn't mean anything to the children, and somehow it fascinates me to consider the Danas playing with my celluloid boat and solemnly splashing each other in their old-fashioned enameled tub.—Why? Have I offended you?"

"I don't think one need get children's thoughts going along that line. And besides, who has any right to know what the Danas, or any couple, may do at home?"

"But, Richie, who knows if what the children said was true or not? They will always say what seems to be expected in the convention of the moment. Cheer up. It meant nothing."

But though I didn't have the word for it then, what I thought was that there was something lightly satanic in his use of other lives, at any age, to amuse him. And yet when I thought of his glowing joy at the company of children, I was ashamed of my qualms, and I lapsed into silence.

[95]

We rose on a long shelf road along the leafy face of the ridge and at the top we doubled back sharply, went down a short slope on the other side, and into our view came the great silent hollow of the quarry.

"What is this!"

"They used to quarry limestone here. Many of our family houses came from this stone. My grandfather owned it and finally closed it down and got a zoning ordinance because he did not want any industrial plants or any organized sort of thing anywhere near the Hills. Our steel mills are the nearest, and they are fourteen miles away, near Calverton. Sometimes at night you can just see the red glow of the furnaces if you look south from Newstead."

The road became a thread of gravel and loose stone. The Isotta skidded and swayed. We went down sharply along the other side of the ridge. A sheer wall fell away from my side of the road straight down to the black water of the quarry lake. Half of the great cavity was in shadow. The walls were three hundred feet high or so, opened out in a great fan shape. Shallow ledges appeared here and there and in their cracks dust had lodged and from the dust green branches grew against the otherwise bare, palatial limestone faces. Our engine made explosive echoes. By their return to us off the opposite cliff we could gauge the size of the quarry— it must have been a quarter of a mile across at the widest point. We scratched and slid our way down the single-track road until we were almost at water level, and there I saw a narrow spit of rocky land which ran out into the lake for a hundred yards. A few bushes clustered along the waterline, and some great blocks of limestone rested like arranged ruins at the far end. We had to leave the car and walk out on the narrow stretch.

"We always called this the Peninsula," said Max. "It was our favorite picnic place. They always made us get out at the top and walk all the way down. Nobody ever has driven down the trail but me."

The day was caught in the silence of the beautifully chiseled cup of the quarry, and the silence seemed intense and sacred—almost as if it could not be broken. Though this was a work of human artisans, the limestone pit seemed to my imagination like some prehistoric natural wonder. The stone cliffs gave off cool air, the winds of the ridge were wafted across and above, and nothing stirred the polished surface of the water. When we spoke our voices took on an added ring. I wondered if there was an echo in the quarry, almost a living spirit.

"Ah, God," said Max, throwing himself down flat to gaze deep into the water at the tip of the Peninsula. Looked into deep down, the water had a midnight-blue color. "This is where I ought to live."

I squinted at him to be sure of my impression. He was like a burdened man from whom cares fell away leaving a brilliant-looking youth whose certainties would take him far.

"We used to keep canoes here when I was little. My father would bring us down here and we would spend whole afternoons on the water."

"Who came?"

"All of us—my sister, my mother, my father, myself, Marietta sometimes." He looked into the water where the past might hang upside down but clear, sweetly colored, untroubled. "We had lovely games. My father and I in one canoe, my mother and Lina in the other. Lina was good with a paddle. My father had us pretend that this was the sea and that we had rival kingdoms on opposite sides. Sometimes we would pay state visits to each other across the sea singing hymns, and other times we had naval battles and tried to tip each other over."

"But wouldn't it be dangerous for children?"

"We swam like fish. If you can believe it, my father was a wonderful swimmer. He taught us early. Lina looked like a watersprite. She could race my father and beat him. He worshipped her. When I was four, she was sixteen. You couldn't think so, but they resembled each other, except that she was blonde like my mother, and Alexander Chittenden has always had dark hair. But Lina was like wheat, silvergold, and as slim, and as pliant, and she was as strong as wire. She could make my father do anything. He loved her but never said so, and when things went wrong for her he tried not to love her any more, but he couldn't stop. The confusion withered him inside and out."

I must have stared at him like a bumpkin. Uncle Alec? He had known hunger and beauty and joy? When? How long ago, before his time of gray and black, with grape-colored stretched lips, and unacknowledged fears which made him hollow within?—he, an exultant young father, making his children a gift of the natural world of water and sky, gaiety and love? Then—I was chastened and ashamed —there was more to see in him than a caricature, as I had seen him?

"Lina. *My sweetling,*" said Max. "He called her that, and I took it up. I used to take my nap with her, insisting that otherwise I could not sleep. I don't know what she ever

[98]

knew about things, but I knew—I knew then as physically as I know now."

"I don't follow you."

"It is bad form to talk about such matters, but I am not famous for my good form. I don't know why, but I can talk to you. Marietta said the same. Anyhow. When I was supposed to be taking my nap with Lina, I lay with my eyes closed and I was like a small cat dozing with love and desire. I held her and she actually slept, but I had a lover's proof of my feeling; my desire was evident to my touch and to my own eye. I wanted her to see and touch, too, but something told me not to let her know. So I made my love to her under the guise of play and teasing. But children can't keep secrets. Maybe nobody can."

"No."

"Anyhow. One day Father somehow saw what was going on. It was the end of my afternoon loving." He paused looking backward in time, and a hard smile rippled over his lips. "I decided long later that he was jealous of me."

"Good God! Your father! Your sister!"

"Yes. Classifications and labels. But as Leonardo pointed out in his notebook, the *verga* lives an independent life, and among other things it ignores are labels and classifications." He sounded like a fallen angel; but if he did not believe in angels, as I was sure he did not, how could he fall? I shook myself away from the idea.

How many first love affairs must happen in the nursery, an Eden that smells of flannel, cocoa, paste, poster paints, and the righteous perspiration of nursemaids.

"But you know?" he said. "I never could be sure that Lina did not know. How could I be sure? They never scolded me or anything, they just separated me and Lina. I had to take naps in the nursery after that, with Nannie sitting by in a rocking chair which squeaked like a mouse. She used to say a rosary under her apron. My family never knew she was a Catholic and I never told on her. One time when I had a high fever she thought I was going to die and she baptized me secretly. When I got well I washed it off with soap, and told her so, but she only smiled mysteriously and looked up to heaven where, by her act of saving me, she felt she was sure to go, bypassing purgatory. When Lina was eighteen she was sent abroad with a maid and a governess to make a tour of Europe in the summer. My father did not want her to go."

Max would overhear discussions between the parents about it. His mother was calm and certain that everything would be all right, after all, they had friends in every city, and Uncle Alec finally consented, provided the foreign agents of his company made a cabled report every day from each city where the travelers paused.

"When she kissed me good-by, Lina cried. Her tears ran into my mouth and I felt desperate with love and lust."

"But a child!" I said, for I had never known of the revelation of the devouring mystery to a young child.

"Yes. And I have often wondered if it would ever have happened so soon with anybody but Lina. —After that, of course, it was bound to happen with someone else, and in a few years, it did."

He looked at me to discover if I knew the one to whom he referred. I was tempted to suffer by a little hot lick of grief at my heart. Was he referring to Marietta? I must not believe so. I had no right to be jealous, but I was. My face told him to keep silent, as I must be silent. I was jealous of love, and of him for having had it since childhood, and of Marietta for her freedom, and of the life they had grown up in together. I took shelter in the ambiguous, and not for the last time in those summer days with that family.

Max turned and yawned to dissipate the threat of revealed emotion.

"So Lina never came back."

"Was that when?" I asked.

"You knew?"

"Marietta told me she married an Italian and had not come home since."

He laughed.

"I have seen her, they couldn't make me not see her. But my father has never seen her since. She made a reasonably happy ending for herself out of what everybody—all my local cousins and the rest—called a scandal. It's not a long story, except that it is, because it is still going on, for her."

One night in Venice there was a great dinner to which Lina was invited. Her chaperon took her to a palace where the feast was spread and came to fetch her at midnight. She was not to be found at first. She had never been as free in her life. She had gone for a small voyage in the gondola of a youth her own age. They fell in love. He had a mistress whom he promised to give up for her. She told him it wouldn't be worth his while as she could only stay in Venice for four days, after which her governess would take her to Vienna. The tour schedule would have to be kept or her father would be distressed. Her friend said four days were an eternity, and much could be accomplished in an eternity. She agreed to let him come to lunch with her at two the next day at her hotel which faced the lagoon and where she had two balconies to choose from. He came, and for the sake of strategy, paid more attention to the chaperon than to

Lina. He was lively and amusing, and though he had no education in the Pennsylvania sense, he seemed to know much about everything that interested Lina. Like someone in a Mozart opera, no, she said long afterward with a husky laugh which suggested endless cigarettes and vats of champagne and frankly comfortable, and transient, infidelities—no, like an earlier Venetian, like Casanova himself, her suitor spirited her away from the Danieli Hotel late in the afternoon. They went to a place he knew and she became his. She stayed with him for two days while the chaperon tried to conceal the loss in order to protect herself; but finally she had to ask a Chittenden representative to come from Milan to help find her, and the lovers were found and unmasked. They were forced to marry, which was not what either of them had in mind, but they were now wildly in love, and they didn't mind marrying. Lina would have to become a Catholic, for her husband's family insisted, and as they were important, they obtained a dispensation from the Cardinal Patriarch for an immediate marriage, with instruction in the Faith to follow. The story had every accent of betrayal in it, and the Chittendens were the victims. Their daughter had broken their hearts, or rather, the once single heart of their marriage.

"That was how Lina became a Principessa," ended Max. "She is still beautiful, but she doesn't look like a gather of wheat any more, but rather like an armful of full-blown peonies with lazy bees drifting over her head. She has a little gesture, as if waving them languidly away now and then. —I met the Prince, later, myself. Lina asked me whom he looked like. I said I didn't know. She said, 'Look again.' I did, and I saw what she meant. He looked like my father as a young man. In old photographs, I mean. You never really *know,* do you."

"Are they happy?"

"You never know, with Europeans, do you. She and her husband are still together. They're not as rich as she would have been otherwise, but people with money like to be seen with them. It is one kind of a career, anyhow."

I was suddenly annoyed by all his yawning worldliness, and I had a hot pit of anger at Marietta in my middle. I would do well not to see her again, I thought. Perhaps she was like Princess Lina, who made love freely. Perhaps Marietta had been making love with Max for who knew how long. But this was my own new love flinching at imagined outrages, and the anger soon dissolved.

"I think we'd better be going," I said. "I am to see your mother at four."

"Our sordid histories depress you," he said. "Very well. Come on."

We went to the car and I had a new grasp of what it meant to drive down the trail instead of walk.

"Where can you turn around?" I asked.

"That's just it. You can't. You have to back up all the way. It is tricky."

Bored by his satisfactions, I had an impulse to walk up the trail rather than ride as he wrangled the Isotta up the sliding gravel incline. But I then thought he would think me afraid, which was what he hoped. I got into the car and as Max took us, jerking and precarious, backwards up the trail, I looked over the deep-shadowed quiet of the man-made crater which seemed like a secret world apart where cares could be lost in memories of better times and human cross-purposes could be dissolved by gazing deep, and wondering what lay at the bottom of the quarry lake.

※ ※ ※

Aunt Lissy's sitting room opened off the corridor near to the great staircase at the center of the house. Her door was open and she was waiting in the hot blurred light of four o'clock. The tall windows were ajar. Their thin curtains drifted in the humid breeze, and I saw her in silhouette with a haze of silver all about her. She was half reclining in a long chair with many cushions. Her fabricated hand rested on a small cushion at her lap. I felt its weight much more there than at the lunch table, where she had supported it with her live hand.

"Come in, Richard. I am expecting you."

She inclined her head toward a deep armchair covered in white linen. I sat down. A sober silence lay between us for a long moment, and then, not knowing what else to do, I smiled. She sparkled her eyes at this and said in a breathy voice which bespoke deep weariness,

"You smile just like Rose. I never thought I'd see her again, but now in a way I have. —Tell me, tell me all about her. Is she well? Your father? Isn't it shameful that I know so little about all of you. But now we know you, Richard, and we feel rewarded."

"I—I yes, well," I said, always confused by compliments face to face, "thank you. Well, my mother is very well, and so is my father. She asked me to remember every little thing here so I could tell her when I got home."

"Does she think of me now and then?"

"All the time."

"You make me feel so remiss—I have not written for ages, and it seemed an inspiration when we thought of asking you to our Fourth of July. Were they pleased to have you come?"

"Oh, yes. They argued and argued with me, and said I would have a wonderful time."

"Ah. You didn't want to come?"

"I am sorry," I said, hot in the face for my tactlessness, "I mean—"

She closed her eyes at me and then opened them with dancing lights set in the twilight of her sorrowful face.

"I know, I know. Some young people dislike any change, and it is all their parents live in hopes of. —But you are I hope having a pleasant time with us?"

"Oh, yes, thank you, yes."

"We all think it such a pity you must leave tomorrow."

I looked glad at the prospect, and she said,

"Will you be eager to get home?"—wistfully, as if to test the possibility that some people really loved to go home, and had a real one to go to.

"Oh, yes."

"You love them."

"Oh, yes."

"Yes, your father was such a handsome man. I was maid of honor, you know? at your parents' wedding. He was full of the most flashing blue-eyed humor that day, he was perfectly certain about everything, and your mother kept looking at him to see what she should do. She was the prettiest human being I ever knew. She was well named. Rose. But still we always called her Kitten because she had such soft brows, and gathered them so often in a look of puzzled interest and charm."

"My mother said she always tried to imitate how *you* looked whenever she wanted anyone to do something for her."

"Oh, no, it was always the other way round. We all tried to talk like Rose, and look like her, and sing like her—she had a lovely voice, you know—and all of us learned from her how to be clever with our fingers." She held my eye with a candid gaze to keep me from glancing down at her lost hand on its cushion. With effort I managed not to look at it. I said,

"She told me to ask you if you remember how dreadfully she behaved at the picnic."

"The picnic?"

"At Lilydale."

"Lilydale. —Oh, my dear. Now I do. Oh, it was priceless." She covered her eyes with her left hand and a whiff of faded laughter rode out on her memory. "It was at the end of our last year in school, we all went on a picnic to the spiritualist colony at Lilydale, near Dorchester, your father was there, and your mother said to him, 'Dan,' she said, 'if you hear me cry out, come in and get me.' —You see we were all going to have a séance with different mediums, all the women had little separate cottages, and your mother went into one of them for a séance, while your father—they were engaged then—while Dan waited behind some lilac bushes outside. Some of us waited with him. Soon we heard a mortal cry coming from the house and Dan dashed in. Your mother was lying on the floor in a dead faint. Dan picked her up and carried her outside. The lady medium followed demanding her three dollars. But your father scolded her for doing anything to make Rose faint dead away. We all cried, 'Doctor, Doctor,' and 'Water, water,' and Dan was so worried he forgot that he was supposed to expect a scream. We began to carry her away, the spiritualist lady went indoors and slammed the door to show what she thought of us, and suddenly Rose with her eyes still closed gave a little coloratura laugh, just like Tetrazzini in *The Barber of Seville,* we all said, and then she leaped out of Dan's arms and stood up and made a deep bow, as if taking a curtain call. The whole scene was staged! Dan turned white with fury. She had made a fool of him, he said, and she said, 'Oh, no, I told you to listen for my cry, I knew all along what I was going to do.' 'No,' he said, he hated to be fooled, especially in front of so many people. —We were all day getting them to make up. Can you believe it? Or do all children dislike to hear anything about their parents from the time long ago when everything was so different? Why are children ashamed of the lives that gave them life?"

To tell the truth, I was embarrassed by the story. How silly of my mother, how boyish of my father, to behave as they did; and worst of all, to keep remembering a thing like that with such self-pardoning happiness.

But Aunt Lissy, telling about it, had grown two little glowing touches of color on her wan cheekbones, and she was stirred by dwelling on a time of love long ago, and her powers seemed to return, so that for a little while she seemed less an invalid. And then she became aware of my stillness which fully expressed my abashment on behalf of my parents for their lost gaieties, and her weariness returned, brought back by my immovable commitment to the present, with all its sorrowful reminders for her. She glanced about the room. All its little pieces of a lifetime's furniture—

framed photographs, objects which were given through the years to mark stages, favorite books each of which retained the time of its first reading, water-color sketches of flowers—condemned her to a present time whose fate she had never expected. She rapidly brushed away unhappy visions with her luxuriant lashes, and said,

"You know, Richard? We have done almost nothing else since you arrived here but talk about you."

"Oh. Then, how?"

"Marietta and I are great friends. We see each other daily, and we chat by telephone also. And my son has indicated his feeling about you, and my husband wrote me a note after lunch saying how much he was taken by your great interest in his library."

I had a sense of an unseen network of information and discussion about me going on everywhere at Newstead. I was uneasy, though vaguely flattered. I had a notion that something was pending—something more than kind sentiments. Aunt Lissy wore a pleading look, as if to say that I must listen patiently, and try to see things her way. She continued in a low voice.

"Max so likes you, Richard. He has told Marietta who has told me. Since you have been here—even this little while—he has been so improved."

"Improved"? Did Max have a "condition"? I had a strike of apprehension.

"Marietta's father does feel he is so very highly strung, we should not be too harsh in our judgments of him when he says or does unkind things. Some days it is very sad and trying." She looked into the future to imagine, like an ailing queen-consort, what the fate of the kingdom must be if the heir were to succeed to it burdened with infirmities which could only mean distress and even ruin for him and for others. Everyone should do the utmost, however awkward and embarrassing, to secure all possible help for him, while there was yet time. "It is difficult to know just how to say what we—Richard, let me be direct. We all think it would be so wonderful if Max could have his cousin with him—you do seem to understand him so well, and it has been years since we have seen him take to anyone as he has to you."

"I like him very much. We seem able to talk."

"Oh, yes."

"Perhaps I could come back sometime, or he could come to visit me."

"Yes, how delightful. But actually, I was thinking of something else—we would of course see that you were not in any way confined, and that you would have time to pursue your own interests, and in fact, though these are difficult things to discuss, a generous allowance would be arranged for you, and you would have as much time to yourself as you might want. . . ."

Could it be that Aunt Lissy was suggesting that I become a member of that household? I was ready to go home, because everything had been planned for that, but I felt a treacherous lick of excitement at the thought of remaining at Newstead—for how long nobody had said—with all its grandeur. It would be like being summoned to Court in France before the Revolution. The strangeness, constraint, and gloom which I had already seen at the heart of the domestic machine of the Chittenden family would surely not reach me, for if I had something they wanted—so ran my swift and greedy thought—they would obtain it by giving me what I wanted, which I could not yet precisely define. Was this what parents meant when they spoke of "going out into the world"? In her anxiety Aunt Lissy could not help pressing her purpose, which, even if in her excitement she thought it original and novel, was common enough; for families with "difficult" children always hope that someone their own age can be acquired to exert "a healthy influence."

"You must not think it odd that there should be such a helpful friendship between two boys such different ages. Max has always been entirely at ease with both older and younger people. And you strike us all as being really: oh very much so: really more mature than your actual age. —What is it again?"

"Seventeen."

"Yes, seventeen. Well, Max is twenty-one; you are both, really, young men. He has lacked real companionship at home for years—except for our darling Marietta, but then a man always needs at least one really good man friend. —You know what would be so splendid? —It would be for you and Max to do a course of reading together, I mean on a regular, daily, disciplined basis. He scatters himself so. He knows everything too easily. He seems to be running from something. We don't know what. Oh, Richard, how beautiful it would be if you could help find it, whatever it is, and help him to face it!"

Her eyes were full of her familiar pale tears caught in the tangle of her lashes. She was waiting for me to say something.

"Yes, it would be, wouldn't it? But he knows much more than I do."

"Perhaps—but what he knows isn't as good as what you know."

"I don't know what that is."

"How to live with what God has given you."

It was true that so far in life I had never had any problem about doing that. Ideas were passing through my mind fast and clear. What did this family hope to acquire in me, what did they hope to take for themselves of what was mine? Perhaps my still unshaken provincialism with its undisturbing values. Perhaps what they thought of as my healthy lack of involvement with tyrannical ideas or persons—since they could not know how my buried wants and wonderings tormented me. Perhaps they thought I could transfer my even temper to the household—but they had never seen me either afraid or triumphant. Did they yearn for my politeness? —How lovely it would be, perhaps they thought, to see some good manners again, and with this hope, they brushed the margins of my parents' lives which spoke through me at my best: my father's confidence in his powers of charm, intelligence, honor, belief in progress, the optimism of Dorchester, a city still innocently growing in all the energetic faith preached by the Chamber of Commerce; my mother's witty gaiety, her intuitive understanding of many umbrageous depths of life's evil underside and the mercy which always showed through her first horror, her innocent avarice for the graces which wealth must surely bring, her wistful hope that her life had been well-used if she had given me to the world (an attitude which weighed upon me), her undismayed acceptance of the years which passed by taking her youth along, and above all, that edifice in life built by my parents together, which consisted of happiness within moderate bounds of material power, sustained by their belief in the forgiveness of sin and their faith in the attainment of heaven.

"What are you thinking, Richard?"

I must have jumped a little in my chair at being brought back by Aunt Lissy's question, and I said,

"Why, I don't know just what you really want of me."

"I was afraid to state it outright to start with, without some little hint of what it would mean to us—what we hope is that you might consent to spend the rest of the summer here, until time for Max to return to Cambridge, and you to go back to school."

"Oh. I see. —I would have to ask my parents."

"Oh, surely, surely—" Her relief was plain as she saw that I did not refuse outright. "We will send a telegram to Dorchester and ask permission to keep you until the first of September. Perhaps your parents could come for a visit just then, and take you home with them. May I tell them you want to stay?"

Now that the first decision was to be made, I felt a qualm, but it seemed impolite to say I wanted to think about it, and I nodded.

"Oh, very good. —And even if they say *No, you must come home,* at least, Richard, you will be here until we have their answer—and that means you may see the night-blooming cereus open! We are all hoping for tomorrow night."

Her animation was charming, and yet there was something feverish in it which made me look away from her white face with its seeking eyes. She added,

"Max will be so pleased."

"Does he know I am being asked?"

"Marietta has mentioned it—*lightly,* I believe, in case of disappointment. —Richard, where do you think we lost him? —No, you have no idea. No. But if you ever find out, do, please, tell us?"

I nodded, glumly inadequate before all such longing ma-
nipulation of human relations. I had a somewhat wild
feeling, caused no doubt by my inexperience, but now I
think I was dimly wondering about the great chain of seeds
by which life is perpetuated, and about how the newly
grown seed claims freedom from its own source and kind.
Such thoughts made my head ache.

"Come here, dear child," said Aunt Lissy, "let me thank
you," and when I went, she lifted her live hand and put it to
my face and traced its contours slowly and gently, in a sort
of kiss by her fingertips, as if to lure forth the tiny unseen
government inside my head which made my kind of life
and character seem so desirable to her and to those who
worked with her to keep hope alive for the future. She
sighed and desisted. I turned to go. She spoke after me.

"Richard, don't get too fond of Max."

I turned to take her meaning. She said nothing further,
but her face was ruefully affectionate—she was so fond of
me, she hoped for so much, that she was warning me that
Max would hurt me if he ever knew he could rely on my
love. It was a marvel that she could make me know this
without telling me in words. Perhaps she even knew how
much I wanted to be like Max—even if it had been possible,
to assume his bodily being, and dazzle the world with it.
Only the great saints are ever free of externals. I was at an
age to live by them in longing and envy.

※ ※ ※

Because the household had to be there early to receive, I saw the party from the first. The Crystal Palace was itself like a great firework laid out in the air, arrested to earth, and sparkling with thousands of lights and their reflections. Green depths within the long glass vaults underlay the glitter, and as night deepened, a row of searchlights laid face up at the edge of the terrace below sent a colonnade of beams straight up into the heavy air. Cars coming on all the valley roads made a web of lights converging on us. Where they came to a halt to deliver their passengers, servants took wraps, and the guests came into the Crystal Palace, across the central court where a fountain kept its plume hovering high under tall palm trees, and out to the terrace overlooking the valley. There in a sort of pavilion made of painted canvas and large flags the family stood waiting to say how do you do. Farther out on the terrace and reaching both ways along its floor were supper tables dressed in bright colors. At each place, party favors commemorating the Fourth of July were laid out—miniature hatchet with a sprig of cherry attached; eagle and shield with the red, white, and blue worked in shiny silk; a tiny trophy of drum, musket, saber, and laurel; and for everyone to wear, a black tricorn hat made of shiny thin cardboard. On a red-carpeted platform against the wall of the greenhouse an orchestra in Continental Army uniforms and white bag-wigs played popular, polite dance music. In a clear space among the tables a dance floor was waiting for the couples who gradually drifted to their places at the tables, only to leave for a few steps before supper. No cocktails were served—only wines at table. Uncle Alec did not believe in Prohibition, but he felt that serving

[114]

mixed drinks before food went too far, and that a law prohibiting this practice would be justified. But no one could ask a handful of friends, as tonight, when he expected a hundred and some guests, without bringing out twenty dozen each of sherry, Pouilly Fuissé, claret, and champagne. Below me three terraces made great steps down the hill front. The second one supported a row of fountains whose basin waters spilled down to the third, which held an illuminated pool of white stone lined with peacock-blue tiling. The fourth terrace was given to grass and plants, and it was there that the fireworks crew were working at the final arrangements for the pyrotechnic concert to come later. I could see the figures of the men—Frazier and others of the staff, and a few boys from their families, in their white shirts with the sleeves rolled up so that they dramatized the style of free citizens on an outing, however much during the rest of the year they were decorously confined in the guise of servants—and I could detect in their movements the controlled excitement they felt for the occasion and the form of celebration they would presently release into the darkening summer sky.

As people arrived, I kept to shadows, for a number of reasons. I knew nobody, everybody sounded intimate with each other and spoke in loud, calm calls which seemed to me like a foreign tongue, they were all older than I, though many were of Max's age, and all were so self-assured that I believed they would look at me with blank politeness and move on, if I spoke to them. And there was another reason —they were all wearing dinner jackets to go with the evening frocks of their girls, and I was outcast by my clothes, for none of Max's had fitted me, and I ended by putting on my Dorchester blue suit, which in drying out under the iron of Max's valet had shrunk enough for me to feel it, though Max assured me after I was dressed that I looked "spiffy."

"But you," I said, when he came to my room to drive me to the party, "why aren't you dressed?"

For he too was wearing a blue suit with a long dark tie, just as I was.

"I thought we'd *both* be different, and tell them to go to hell if they didn't like it," he said, with a general smile of rebellion which made him my accomplice in bumpkinry.

"You didn't have to do that," I said.

"Don't be proud," he said. "If it suits me to do it, I do it, and vice versa. The funny thing is, they'll pretend not to notice, but they'll all mention it to each other. Let's go."

He was right, for as people came down from the receiving line, I could see them indicating Max with a glance or a wave, and laughing over him. I had a leap of belief that later when they should happen to notice me, the visiting cousin, dressed as outlandishly, they would suddenly decide that it was really quite distinguished of the two of us to set our own style.

I kept watching for Marietta to arrive with her parents. I had been feeling a strange knot of resentment and excitement about her since the afternoon; but now, alone in this loud and alien throng, I longed for her; and so my eye was on the pavilion most of the time. My cousins were now in their public character, and I could only admire it. Uncle Alec, in his old-fashioned tuxedo that was a bit more loose on him with each passing year, looked, from my distance among the tubbed trees on the terrace, whiter and more frail than before, but his smile was flashing, as he made his birdlike lifts and turns, and his glasses winked, his high handshake with his elbow up seemed like an accolade, and now and then a fragment of his welcome came to me in a sort of stylish shriek which made others turn and laugh, and say, "Alexander is really marvelous tonight," so indicating that his general incapacity was well known, but in a sense admirable, if he could work it up to such a party as this, in such idle magnificence, with such dynastic implications.

For his wife standing beside him was, if you watched from a little way away, for all to recognize the perfect consort for a reigning house. She too was pale, but the fall of light from overhead modeled her with such strong relief that her famous beauty came back upon her, and as she felt that it was being seen again by others who had almost forgotten how beautiful she had been, she was given strength to stand so beautifully erect, to offer a smile so general that was yet taken so particularly, to give her hand so fondly that nobody noticed at the time which hand it was. She wore white kid gloves that reached above her elbows. Her right arm was suspended in a sling of black lace and hung heavily at her waist; but in the lace she had twined a long chain of small diamonds—far from attempting to conceal her deformity she called attention to it by this device, and pleased everyone by putting them at ease to notice the sling and its jewels which as she moved winked like fireflies inside the cloudy lace. Her dress was white, long, and shimmering. She had obeyed her husband to the extent of celebrating the day by wearing a string of rubies, below which was a string of white pearls, which was supported by a string of sapphires. Guests could exclaim at the wit of this, and use their time with her by doing all the talking themselves, which spared her saying much herself, so saving her strength. How wonderful they are together, was what many of them said, seeing with what animation Alexander would relinquish a guest to her, and how she would thank him with a sparkle of her eyes as she accepted her charming duty, and then, how, leaning sweetly to remind Max who it was he must now welcome in his turn, she would make the word "darling," which she meant to be overheard, seem to include playful love as the open secret of motherly pride, and an adult gaiety which took the guest in for tonight as one of the family. It was hard to remember the exhausted and troubled lady whom I had been with at four o'clock that afternoon.

Max in public himself was all she could ask, as he took one after another of the guests in his turn. I was reminded of my first glimpse of him—how he leaned a little forward, his glowing face turned to seek in other faces the nature of their desires, which he would promptly meet—and in certain cases of the old and corrupt or the young and eager who came this evening he would (unspokenly) suggest desires of his own, and invite excesses in their thoughts which if they should ever be revealed he would then laugh at.

While I was observing him from an orderly thicket of tall plants, where spokes of shadow wheeled across the terrace cast by figures that moved in the crowd, a voice said near to my ear,

"I don't know how much longer he can stand it."

I turned.

"Marietta. I was watching for you."

"I came around the other way. I never go down the receiving line."

"They are all being splendid, aren't they?"

"Lissy loathes to be seen, and this means she must put herself for all to see. You know what the locals in society call the Chittendens? They call them the Imperial Family."

"You look lovely."

"A junior hag," she said.

"Oh, no."

"Oh, yes. I am exhausted. Always. Don't I look it?"

In the flickering half-light of the party, I regarded her. Her face was pale, her eyes were deep under her brows, and her face narrowed about her smiling lips which quivered in a tiny spasm now and then. Somehow this suggested wit. She looked ghostly and lovely, in spite of the remote reminders she again gave me of the look of a skull, and of consuming appetite the nature of which was ambiguous, except that the working flare of her nostrils suggested the perennial presence of desire. Unlike the other girls at the party, who wore modish knee-length frocks weighted with crystal fringes and bangles, she was dressed in a long close gown of light silk patterned in leaves and branches of several shades of green, so that her thin, eager, restless figure seemed to be entangled in a thicket of vines. Her hair fell loose on her bare shoulders. She looked small and vital, and I wanted to enfold her protectively with my arms, as if she were an exquisite child escaped from the nursery in her warm, trailing nightgown. With her knack of catching a thought and talking in refraction, she said,

"You are going to save us all. I am so glad, the telegram has been sent."

"You mean to my parents?"

"Yes."

"You know all about it."

"All."

"Does Max?"

"No—only that you were going to be asked. Are you pleased?"

"I—"

"You don't know. You rather hate the feeling that some-one is buying you. But you see what is needed and you feel you might do some good. And we are all strange but interesting, and one can learn something from any situation. You half hope they will say no at home, but if they say yes, you won't be sorry. Perhaps this will be a summer you will think of as memorable. But you cannot help the notion that there is something a little unwholesome about having so many odd new friends wanting something they think you can give them." She shrugged. "Or don't you want to talk about it?"

"No, I don't."

"Oh, Richie, as Max calls you, you are priceless. I adore you when you look lofty. It means you are puzzled but refuse to admit it. Do you want to dance? Or be dragged around to meet people?"

"Let's dance."

We moved to the dance floor where she hung upon me, yet not close to me, stepping shortly in her own rhythm, and not facing me but swaying limply at right angles to me. In an elusive way, she was like a small wild creature under restraint. Friends called to her and she flickered at them with the fingers entwined in my hand. The party was suddenly complete. We saw the Imperial Family come down from their place and move slowly to their tables. It was a signal for the dancing to stop and everyone to be seated. Uncle Alec presided at one round table, Aunt Lissy at another, Max at another where places for myself and Mari-etta were arranged with her between us. Three other couples completed the table. I was not introduced to any of them.

"Oh," said a ripe, brunette girl in a throaty voice, "let's all be George Washington," and put on her tricorn hat. Every-one glanced at Max. He nodded and put on his hat, at which everyone else did so. Marietta put her fluttering hand on Max's arm.

"I *know,*" she said, "but it can't last forever. They love it. You're being superb."

"Richie, am I?" he said, leaning across her toward me.

"If you are," I said, "I don't know what about."

Max and Marietta sighed in concert at my insensitivity.

"Isn't it all divine?" said another girl who sat at my right. I turned. She was an enthusiastic blonde with a permanent smile and a clear, lifted voice in which she drawled her remarks, carelessly confident that they would be of interest to everyone. "I mean, the Alexanders really are something, don't you think? I mean, who else gives such divine parties. I have never seen you here before. Who are you?"

"I am a remote cousin of this family. I have never been here before."

"Where are you from?"

"Dorchester."

"Delaware?"

"New York."

"Oh, *there.* Good heavens above. Do you hear?" she said generally, while others turned to hear her. "He's from Dorchester, New York. Can you bear it? We had a girl from Dorchester, New York, at school, for a short while. Nobody could understand a word she said. She was a pretty little thing, too. She had to leave us because she didn't care for horses—or perhaps it was the other way round."

"Gwennie, you're awful," said a boy across the table.

"I know, and you love it," she replied. She turned and pointedly looked at my suit. "Love your suit," she said.

"And Max's?" asked Marietta, suddenly appearing to her. As she stretched to speak she leaned against me and I could feel her deep quivering energy.

"Oh, and Max's, naturally," said Gwennie. Then she turned away to her partner on the other side.

"Thank you," I said to Marietta.

"She had to be sent packing. Let's us three just make social noises at each other."

Max looked at me with his head lowered. For the benefit of the party he retained his smile. But for me he had a simmering gaze which silently said what he must not say aloud.

"Absolutely *divine*," came at random over the shoulder on my right.

The party was now fully launched.

❧ ❧ ❧

Max took Marietta to dance. I kept my seat. Presently Gwennie turned to me again.

"I'm a dreadful bitch, don't you think?"

"If you think so."

"Oh, come *on*. React."

"There's not much point."

"I suppose not. What do you do, at college, I mean."

"I am in my last year of school. I plan to take a pre-medical course."

"My dear. I took you for a college man. *Now* won't you forgive me?"

"Why do you want me to?"

"Very well. If you won't keep it *social,* I'll tell you.

Because you are a cousin of Max's, and that means we really ought to be nice to you, because if Max ever gets mad at anyone they have an awful time making up with him, and I *like* being asked here, and my mother would snatch me *bald* if I ever did anything to make trouble for any of us with the *Alexanders*. So now you know why I took any more trouble with you, and now I suppose you will tell Max anyway, so why should I ever *not* be a bitch?"

I laughed out loud at this, and I remember thinking what a remarkable report I could take home to my friends about how children of the rich behaved at Chittenden Hills.

"No," I said, "I won't tell Max anything."

"Say, you're a real prince of a fellow," she said, burlesquing an innocent air. "—Did you know they're engaged?"

"Who."

"Then you don't. Max and Marietta. My mother—all the old people—have been told quietly this evening. No formal announcement. Just intimate family news. No wedding, of course, until after Harvard."

"I see."

"Do you like her?"

"Oh, yes."

"Yes, I can see you do. You really open up to her, don't you? I mean, it's how you look when you talk to her or she talks to you. I can tell by the back of your head."

"You ought to take it up professionally."

"Now who's a bitch."

I was beginning to like her. She thrust and invited, she was working so hard to put forward her own idea of herself, and her inverted style of offensive attention was in the end flattering, as she meant it to be.

The music was slowing to a pause between dances. Max and Marietta returned. She said,

"Gwennie, let him alone. He belongs to us."

I think now of the reflected meanings of this, none of which were consciously intended; but at the time, all I felt was a little chill of apprehensiveness at the note of possession, and I dreaded to know how my parents would reply to the telegram which asked for me. Gwennie ignored Marietta and made a kiss through the air to Max and turned back to her other dinner companion.

"Dance with her," said Max, handing Marietta to me.

"You might let him ask," said Marietta.

"No," I said, "I was going to."

As we went to the dance floor Max took his way off between the tables, turning and twisting among them and pausing as arms and smiles went out to him. He had a word for each, and a kiss here and there, and beyond, I had a shuttered impression of his mother's face, watching him fearfully between the heads and bodies whose relation to him, and to her, and to us on the dance floor, changed as he moved, and we. Aunt Lissy's head was held beautifully erect and her throat was stretched in a regal pose so that a casual glance would seem to collect an impression of a reserved but serenely confident and happy lady of great position enjoying with her devoted husband and her handsome, gifted, and adoring son a simple meeting of friends to observe Independence Day. Banking upon their long history, the Chittendens could be pardoned for making something of a proprietary reference to the Revolution, in terms beyond the appropriate privileges and material means of most others.

We danced a little while more or less on the same spot of the dance floor in obedience to Marietta's habit of ignoring the rhythm, the movement, and the idea of dancing. She said,

"It is idiotic, isn't it."

"What."

"The idea of dancing. I mean people on their hind legs going around face to face in couples to noises made by other people to keep them moving all the same way. I never do."

"I've noticed."

"Let's go and be somewhere."

Holding my hand she took me away to the end of the terrace where high stone urns held flowering bushes whose branches showered down to the terrace floor. In the shadow of one of the urns we sat on the wide balustrade looking out over the valley. Fireflies defined a low ceiling over the meadow floor with their little lost and found lights. The dance band was muffled at the small distance where we were. The dense summer night seemed to have its center in my belly. I was choked with anticipation of I knew not what. The air was heavy and sweet. Down in the valley, with the power to hurt which is part of any universal banality, the lights in Mr Standish's house looked somehow promising and dear, making me wish I had a house with windows lighted at night against the impersonal dark, while inside the house might abide my life with someone I loved.

Marietta took my hand and made her butterfly touch on my upturned wrist. I was flooded with desire and my pulse leaped in my wrist and made me shift my thighs.

"Oh, it is lovely," she said.

"Marietta."

"I mean, to have it respond that way."

I think it was in that moment that I first knew how desire reached outward as well as inward. I took her in my arms. She flinched away into nothing and turned her head away.

"Oh, Richie, let's wait. Nothing is clear."

I held her and then let go. The night was heavy on us again. She breathed in a loud whisper and shook her head and made a groan of longing under her breath.

"What's the matter," I said.

"The same thing. Always."

"Max?"

"Yes. —Richie, what can I do when things engulf him until he has to disappear for a day or a night?"

"What does he do?"

"He says he cannot help it, he does not know what causes it, he does nothing, he just sits somewhere or lies on something, and the tears run down his face. He does not even weep, I mean, with noises and things. But something inside breaks like a dam, or a heart, or something, and he cannot stand anything for a while, but all he can do is be a part of some sorrow of the whole world. And so young! Like tonight. You know? When he left us?"

"But he seemed to be having a beautiful time."

"Oh. It was nearly killing him."

"The party?"

"All of it. Everything. And especially his family."

"But they seem happy."

"Oh, Richie. It is just because you are generally happy. Everyone else seems happy to you. I hope you can always stay that way."

"I'm not any way, particularly."

"Oh, yes you are, and I adore it; but I know more about it than you."

"Can't you help Max?"

"I keep thinking so. I used to be able to, at first, but when he began to see that things were not going to be good again, nothing seemed to help him. We've tried lots of things. You're the latest."

"We?"

"Oh, yes. I keep having ideas."

"Did you tell them to keep me?"

"Yes. —D'you mind? Oh, don't, please, mind. I was so— so desperately pleased when I saw how Max took to you. If you knew. He hasn't taken up anybody new in ages. —Oh, but how can I make you see. Even this, now, with you—he is furious at me underneath because he *knows* without being told that I have tried to give you to him. He hates to be managed, he knows he needs it, and what he misses most is the joy of discovery. Perhaps I have made a dreadful mistake."

"About me?"

"Yes. Perhaps he should have been left to make you love him."

"Oh, I never heard so much talk about love."

"But, darling Richie, all this is about that, and nothing else. In fact, that's all anything is ever about, if you look far enough."

I was so much stirred by this that I must pretend not to be, and so I said,

"It doesn't sound quite decent, to me. Are there no things you won't talk about?"

She sighed and set her head against my arm, like a wishful child.

"It is talk or go mad," she said. "If I had one wish for us all here in the Hills it would be that we would never want to look past the surface of things. That is what is killing Max—feeling and knowing things under the grand outsides of the life he comes from."

"What outsides?"

"Oh: surely you know. His non-father, and his crippled mother. The loss of everything too soon. We are all going to lose everything, but most of us have a chance to get ready. He didn't. —He has such doubts. He remembers such happiness."

"I know. He told me about when he and his sister were young, and his father, and the games they played at the quarry. Uncle Alec was evidently quite a man in those days."

"Oh, yes. Even I can remember. Alexander was a darling —so handsome and such imagination and so much fun. The clever thing to say around here is that Lina murdered him. And when Alicia needed him, he was dead, and he couldn't"—shrug—"anything. And Max lost the mother he knew, and so he has to hate her for it, and of course everybody else, and himself, and everything about his life, and this party, and those Gwennies and Sonnies and Didis and Tooties and Poopsies over there dancing. —My father told me all this. I am too dumb to know it by myself. Aren't you sorry you ever came?"

"I didn't want to."

"I know. I adore the terrible candor of the provinces."

"That's not very nice."

"We don't have to be nice, do we?"

"Not if you're rich enough, I suppose."

"Oh, Richie, I have made you cross. I am sorry. My father

told me years ago to begin by saying half as much as I'd like to. And then to cut what was *left* in half, if I ever wanted to be liked."

"It's all right."

But I was made forlorn by a memory of the city which had shaped my life, Dorchester, of which my father approved so warmly and innocently; and when it was made fun of, as vaudeville comedians always did to raise a sure laugh, I was indignant. I wondered what was so funny about being born in a city in Upstate New York, at the other end of things from New York City, and I would think hotly that people in New York City and Dorchester were both people, and I would ask what could be so different about them? But tonight there were differences to be seen, and these were too new for me to know how I felt about them. That they existed was enough of a shock. I kept silent, watching the lovely net of firefly lights far below. The dance band went silent, too, and in the pause, I heard another sound—drifting under the low clouds from the fold of the hills it was the whistle, given in long phrases, of the night freight train downbound to Olympia. It had a sort of rainy sound, for the night was humid and the air pressed close.

"Oh, how beautiful," said Marietta. "I love to hear it and feel sad—it is so wonderful to have something *there,* and not *here,* to be sad about."

"Let's stop being sad," I said, happy that we had come together again.

And as if in reply to my words, just then, from the lowest terrace below us, with a hissing chord of fiery power into the sky rose a golden curtain of sparks made by the exhausts of twenty rockets which went up in a long row at the same instant. Startled, the guests all gave out a great chord of their own, crying "Oh-h-h!" in a sustained sigh of enchantment. The curtain rose to a ragged edge across the sky, there was an instant of darkness and silence, and then the rockets burst in a line, throwing firelights of green, red, yellow, and rose, which exploded to release showers of diamond white needles falling back from the apex like spray of fountains or fronds of willow trees against the dense summer night. The concert immediately cast a spell against whose dazzle of glory no one who watched could maintain, while it lasted, any visions of his own, especially those which fed on darkness or sorrow. In their act of enchantment supremely innocent, fireworks restored innocence, for the moment, to anyone who watched them.

※ ※ ※

How suddenly a rocket went out at the end of its glory; and how craftily Uncle Alec's crew timed the elements of the display so that there was hardly a pause between one glory and the next. The concert was to last an hour, and for the time I saw of it the heavens were never dark, and there were few outright repetitions of effects. Salutes exploding on high had their bombardment doubled by the echoing hills, and when these were topped by falling stars of red fire we thought of battles and patriots. Arbors of green arcs were woven in the sky, and in turn these were pierced by hissing comets which streaked aloft and still climbing died in wafts of golden sparks which fell slowly into nothing. Gardens of immense gold chrysanthemums were planted high over the meadow—bursts of curly light all radiating from a sun which burned the dark and then joined it. Pagodas rose crown by crown, and in the little pause before each stage took fire, we chanted "Oh-h-h-h" in chorus, and our voices rose each time a new shaft grew from the last, and we ached with delight at how the splendor was protracted, and when at last the pagoda was finished, we still held our breath, thinking another climb and burst would surely come. But before we could measure disappointment, something else went up, and took us with it.

The greatest rockets were those which on reaching the apex made a great soft sound something like a kiss, and then released their fronds of light in falling traceries which seemed to me like a picture of the very nerve tree within the human body. Having it made visible in fancy was like suddenly feeling everything everywhere at each nerve end, a sensation mercifully brief, for its intensity and wholeness must have been impossible to bear for long. Our very flesh was pierced by those threads of light, and we possessed glory and color as part of our being.

I looked about at the rapt faces and tense positions of the guests. I was struck by a notion which, I am sure, would never have come to me at home at such a moment. I thought of what pathos attended the need and fulfillment of play. Playgrounds and amusement parks, fireworks and games, all seemed pathetic monuments to human desperation. Why must our lot be made bearable by spectacle, and what must it be if the longing to be delivered from it even briefly was so constant? How much better, for the most part, people deserved in the way of relief from their human estate than what they were given, usually at considerable expense.

"Oh-h-h-h!" we said again, as the darkness was made bright by a great rise of whirling discs in every color. They filled the sky and seemed to fly away to infinity, growing smaller and yet brighter, until, mere sparks, they seemed to part an invisible curtain and enter another sky where we could not follow.

❧ ❧ ❧

We were holding hands as we watched when Max suddenly stood behind us and leaned over between us.

"Let's all get away from here," he said in an urgent whisper.

We turned. In the light of the fireworks he looked to be carved out of marble. Marietta groaned and put her hand on his face.

"What do you mean," she said.

"We've had enough."

"Yes, of course, though it is lovely. But we can't leave."

"Why not."

"It would look dreadful. It would hurt Alicia. This is supposed to be *our* party."

"Yes. I give it away freely."

"I cannot go. If you want to, go. But I must stay and handle things if people ask for you."

"Come along, Richie," he said, disdaining further discussion. Confident that I would follow, he started toward the steps leading down from the terrace away from the tables. I looked at Marietta.

"Oh, go," she said. "If it wasn't this, it might be something worse. Bring him back in an hour or so."

Feeling that my duties had already begun, I followed Max

down the steps, around the grassy hump beyond the Crystal Palace, and down the driveway until we came to his car. He drove without lights until we were headed away from the Crystal Palace along the quarry road. I was full of things to ask which Max would hate to answer. Feeling this, he drove in silence, refusing to break the wall of privacy which contained him.

The headlights were now turned on, and he drove fast. We rapidly closed on Mr Standish's cottage. I saw and was about to exclaim a warning of what Max saw in the same moment. Standing in the middle of the road, watching us bear down on him, was Chief, the Dalmatian.

"God damn them," cried Max, braking hard, "they're not supposed to let him out!"

Before we skidded to a halt, the dog was dancing alongside our right front wheel trying to bite the tire.

"Careful!" I yelled, "you'll run over him!"

"That's all I need!" exclaimed Max. He jumped from his seat and his dog rose to dance his old dance with him but Max cuffed him down, grasped his collar, and led him through the picket gate to the cottage. There he pounded angrily on the door. I saw a woman's shadow slowly and heavily move on to the frosted glass door panel, and then the door opened. I could not hear what they said, only the blur of their voices. With irritating calm the woman—it was Mrs Standish—took the dog by his collar and drew him into the house, a process which he made as awkward as possible by relaxing into a dead lump of weight. Max returned now freed into speech by his encounter with the gardener's wife.

"The silly cow. What horrors that sort of women are. She thinks it vulgar to do what she is paid to do." He started the car and we were off again. He imitated the woman's bridling whine. "It wasn't her fault. It wasn't Standish's fault. There is a hole under the fence of Chief's pen which they'd been meaning to fill up, but what with Mr Standish, she called him The Mister, being off at all hours in the greenhouse watching for that thing to bloom, and herself so busy around the house, they never—and my! aren't the fireworks just so pretty, she was watching from her bedroom window, and she thought she heard a knock, and so she came to see. —She thinks she will cease to be a lady if she ever admits she's been wrong about anything. Poor Standish. Anyway, she promised to keep Chief in the house till they get the hole filled. My poor dog, living with that sagging slut."

"Max, Max."

" 'Max, Max,' yes, yes. I know."

We came to the ridge and climbed the chattery road. At the top I said,

"We'd better walk down."

"Scared?"

"No."

He turned toward me with a calculating grin, moving his jaw slowly. By the light of the instrument panel he could see that I was not scared. He laughed and said,

"I believe you. Then we'll walk. I only drove back up once after dark and I actually did run the rear wheel off the edge. They had to come and haul me back onto the road."

He left the car on the ridge. With a flashlight he took from under the seat he showed our way down to the quarry lake. We walked out to the point of the Peninsula and climbed up on the limestone blocks which looked like architecture. From there, the air was black, the high chiseled walls blacker, and the water blacker still. It took minutes for my eyes to become adjusted to the cup of darkness where we were, and all seemed quiet. But slowly the senses reached for the world outside, and I could see, as though I were pressing upon my eyes with the lids shut, a wavering faint glow in the far sky, a wash of light cast on the low clouds by the fireworks four or five miles away. I watched hoping to see a rocket reach its dying height above the quarry walls so far above us; but never did. And too, in the quiet I began to hear the faintest reduction of the explosions from the airy salutes at Newstead, and then nearer to us I could hear the murmur of summer creatures, an occasional flap and splash of a fish, and the threading song of distant crickets. A great trembling seemed to hover above the stillness which was made of so many combined live sounds. By the contrasts slowly made manifest in sky and air, the lake seemed to be deeper and darker than ever, a pool of oblivion, a world nowhere and welcoming, to a self lost and searching.

We sat in silence for perhaps a quarter of an hour. Was I supposed to break the quiet? "How peaceful," I might say— but though I could hardly see him, my cousin beside me was held by anything but peace, for if he was silent, he seemed to be using silence as a refuge from powers which menaced him from within and without. How was I supposed to help him? How could I know what he wanted not of me so much as of his life? At last I heard him move—I could hear the small moist sound of his eyes as he rubbed them roughly. When he spoke it was with his familiar air of mockery but his voice was choked.

"When was the last time *you* shed tears?" he asked with almost a dry, professional inflection.

"I would have to remember."

"Tell me why you did, and where. How long ago?"

"It isn't very interesting."

"Never mind. Go on."

"Why, I think it was two years ago when I broke my arm tobogganing in Commodore Perry Park. The run was icy and I missed a turn and flipped over. It was when they picked me up. It hurt so that I couldn't help it, I felt the tears running down my face and I couldn't stop them for several minutes. But finally I did."

"You are right, it is not very interesting. You were not really *shedding tears* about something. Physical pain is of no importance."

"I suppose not. But you asked me."

"Yes, I asked you. And I have asked others. And nobody can tell me."

"Max?"

"Yes?"

"What is it?"

A pause. Then,

"Are you going to stay?"

"Oh. I won't know until I hear from my parents."

"Do you like them?"

"Yes, I do."

"Do you want to stay?"

"Partly yes. Partly no."

"A just reply, most potent, grave, and reverend signior. I could phrase it better, but the substance is surely proper. —Do you hate beauty?"

"Good God, of course not."

"Do you hate staying well by keeping busy?"

"God, I don't know."

"Don't be impatient. These are great questions. And so is this one: do we find true happiness only when we live **for** others without regard for self?"

Mocking the precepts played at him at home in that house of invalids, he was trying to show me something of life which unless it engulf him he must despise, and despising, fight against. He talked on in the darkness. His thoughts were not consecutive, but they were all radial to his central unhappiness, about the nature of which there were many theories but no proofs.

Doctor Osborne had used his privilege of old retainer now and then to advise Max to seek professional help for his "nerves." But Max told him that he felt intelligent enough to find his own cure for what ailed him. Doctor Osborne sighed and disagreed, knowing what he knew, but not risking any direct reference to it, and aside from keeping a keen eye on him, he let Max alone, obviously waiting for the moment when Max would no longer be able to make a show of rationalized resistance. Meanwhile, though he was willing to let Max and his daughter be the closest of companions, he withheld his approval of an official engagement—hence tonight's seepage of romantic information through the medium of matronly gossip. In due course if all went well with Max he would be happy to bless the union. But not yet. Not yet. The idea occurred to Max that Doctor Osborne was entertaining in thoughts to which he denied full daylight the idea that time and mortality would resolve Max's difficulty. When he came into his inheritance, when his parents died, when he need not hate what he loved too well in memory, Max would probably be fully one man instead of a collection of fragments from his own childhood, and from the youth of his parents, and from the bored, fastidious, languid, but brilliant Max of Harvard. People went to such lengths to "understand" him that they ended by misunderstanding him into unreality. The black water in the quarry, whose every rock and ledge and face he knew so well above the water, held depths he could only imagine. Did they only mirror what was above? How would he ever know? When did his life turn into an eternal question, while the lives of other young men seemed arrogantly and joyfully to be certain, however wrongly, only of answers?

I heard a reflection of his voice in that rocky cup. I asked, "Is there an echo here?"

"Ai, God," he said. Then in a deliberately restrained voice he said, "When we were little we talked to it all the time. We never saw it, but we knew it lived here, and we used to think of things to ask it. It always answered. If you want to hear it, I can summon it up for you. —All right." He stood up and drew a deep breath, and then in a tremendous voice, he cried out one word four times, lengthening it as far as his breath would let him:

"Howl, howl, howl, howl!" —and the great palatial rocky walls threw it back at us and then echoed their own echo, and I heard "Howl—owl—owl—wl—l . . ." and though I did not then know where his word had come from, it plumbed me with a weight of dread which pressed my heart down, down.

When the echo had returned to the silence where it lived, we said nothing for a moment, and then Max said,

"Do you want to try it?"

"No, thanks."

"No, there is little use. All you discover is that every question is finally its own answer."

It was the kind of remark which meant nothing or everything, and I was not at ease with such. Kindly accepting my silence,

"Smoke?" he asked, taking his cigarettes and a briquet from his pocket.

"No, thanks."

"You don't ever?"

"No."

He lighted his cigarette. His shapely head bent over the flame, his high color, the tawny marble of his hands carved out by the brief light, gave a picture of such fine health that I was startled, for what he had been trying to say for so long and dark an interval had made a different likeness of him— that of an invalid being drawn helplessly into the illness all around him, which he had helped to create.

"Why don't you smoke. Do you disapprove?"

"No, I don't disapprove. Years ago, my father promised me a thousand dollars when I reach twenty-one if I promised not to smoke until then. I promised."

"So now," said Max to whom a thousand dollars was not a fortune, "you don't want to lose a thousand dollars?"

"It isn't the thousand dollars, though I can't sneer at it as you can. But what I don't want to lose is my promise."

My cloddish virtue exasperated him, with its terms of innocence and honor. He said, envious of the settled simplicity of my life,

"How do you know your father will keep his? Great God, haven't you ever taken a straight look at life? Don't you know even yet that nothing is what it seems to be? When are you going to wake up?"

But under his words something else said: Richie, Richie, don't ever wake up; and I knew long later that the very thing everyone hoped to purchase of me for Max was that part of my father and mother's abiding faith which I carried in me—their faith in whatever it was which created instead of destroyed.

"If my father is alive when I reach twenty-one, he will keep his promise," I said.

"Ah, God," he said, cast down even further by what he had not credited me with—the ability to contemplate with calm, though surely never to experience without grief, such a catastrophic event as the death of the father. If Max was frantic as we escaped from the fireworks party—"festival for the peasants," he had said—now he seemed deeply depressed by his conversation with me, which was just the opposite of what was supposed to come from our healing contact. He sat and smoked in silence with his head turned away until his cigarette was gone. Then abruptly he stood up and began to haul off his clothes.

"Let's take a swim," he said.

"I'll wait for you."

"You don't want to?"

"Not specially."

"The water is cold."

"Yes. It isn't that. I'd rather just sit here and feel the night."

My flesh threw out goose pimples and my teeth made as if to chatter, but I bit my jaws together. It was a close, hot night. How could I shiver?

"Then a good night to you," he said, and dived off the great limestone cube and vanished into the black. Would he come back? I asked myself, and then I recoiled from the question, asking why anything like that should ever occur to me.

The summer night pulled all the rankness of the countryside into the heavy air. I listened for water sounds but heard
nothing. Across the quarry rim the distant lights came and
went in the sky but gave no illumination here. It was like
seeing the dying flicker of a hearth fire gone so low that its
last cast of color was not rosy but wan pale. The fall of
another coal or two, a final spark, and all would be dark. I
thought of calling out his name, but for fear of seeming
foolish if he should answer, I kept silent. I held my breath to
hear without the drumming of my pulse. Somewhere an
owl spoke—a small one, by the sound. What would they say
if I returned without him? First I must find Marietta and if
necessary put my hand over her mouth to keep her from
crying out when I told her my news. Then we would have
to find a stratagem to take Alexander and Alicia away from
the terrace party without having anyone notice anything.
Could we say that the head gardener wanted them briefly in
the Crystal Palace, perhaps because the night-blooming
cereus was showing signs of movement in its folded buds?
And then beyond the crowd of guests, we would go in a
motorcar back to the hilltop house, and there my duty
would end with the news I brought. Surely it would be wise
to ask Doctor Merriman Osborne to be with us at that
moment. Nobody would shed tears but Uncle Alec, who
would turn his narrow head aside and extending his long
neck in birdlike thrusts, would then release a series of
broken dry sounds which would sound more like illness
than grief. A few cars would presently come up the driveway with people who would want to know if anything was
wrong. What instinct would have brought them? A word

would have to be sent at once to the estate work force to go to the quarry with lights, ropes, a boat, a Pulmotor, perhaps a salute cannon to fire across the water in classical fashion to bring up by its vibrations any burden held by the deep. Such activity would be impossible to conceal. In an instant the entire throng of guests would have the news, and face each other with it in horror and excitement. How could it possibly have happened? He had been such a superb swimmer—so excellent that, because of his prep school record in the pool, he had been asked at Harvard to join the varsity squad, which he had disdained to do. Someone was sure to say that something like this could have happened all through the years, the quarry lake had long been a menace, and nobody had heeded warnings that it should be drained and dried up for good. Over Newstead and its impregnable evidences of great position the fates would seem to be gathered, as if one success in calamity after another deserved still another. How would it be possible to look into Aunt Lissy's face as she was turned and taken up the long winglike curve of the grand staircase to her room and ultimate solitude? Before daylight the reporters and photographers would be everywhere. The efficient apparatus of disaster would come into play for the satisfaction of all who could read.

I could not be still with my racing thoughts. I clambered down from the blocks and tiptoed—why I tiptoed I did not know—feeling my way to the edge of the Peninsula as if to see and hear better. I felt like a prisoner in a palatial dungeon whose invisible chains were made of darkness itself. But where was the flashlight? I returned to the rocks and felt for it everywhere but could not find it. I did not know whether five minutes had passed or a half hour. I looked across the lake toward the opposite limestone wall. If I called out my voice would echo strongly, and surely there would be an answer from some quarter of the sheer cavity? Then I saw a long edge of most dim pale light along the top of the wall. It revealed the crest, and as I watched transfixed, it traveled with breathless slowness down the limestone face, throwing into dark relief against the stone the occasional ledges where foliage had rooted and grown in a wonderful persistence of life out of siftings of dust caught in invisible crevices. I turned, and there over the other crest was rising a hazy quarter moon which as it rose sent its light down the far quarry wall and must eventually show it all, and touch the water. How long this would take I could not calculate, but my entire will was bent to join the rising of the moon, as though I could hasten its movement, for if there was light, however remote and confusing, I would not feel buried in mystery and solitude.

"Yes," I said aloud, in an idle tone calculated to sound reassuring, "perhaps it is time to go."

I turned my head to listen for a reply. None came. My body seemed compact of a silent groan which if it could have been heard would have said, "No, no, no, please."

I went to the blocks, climbed up, and lay down on my back to watch the sky and the moon. I was trapped with them in the inexorable design of the passage of the heavenly bodies. Like the heavy air itself, my underthoughts hung under a misting atmosphere of dread into which flickers of reasonableness tried to penetrate. But like the shadows in the summer undergrowth at night, everything conscious within me merged into a single depthless form, which slowly made itself felt as a knot of suspense and desire, hunger and shame—for what, except for life itself, I could not say. Later,

I knew how any extreme of feeling—grief, rage, relief—could find expression, however inappropriate it might seem at the moment, in an act of sex.

I suddenly sat erect.

What sound was that—what touched the water with a little slap?

I turned my head. I heard it again. Then I heard the long luxurious indraught of the swimmer lazily rolling aside for his breaths in an Australian crawl of, surely, perfect form. It was my cousin returning. I felt a thump of relief in my chest, immediately followed by a prickling gather of anger. My wild concern, with its ceremonies of the imagination, now seemed childish and idiotic. I was humiliated by it. Before I would let it show to Max, I would perjure myself. I lay back on the rock and rolled to my side and curled myself in a position of sleep, and pretended to be asleep when he climbed up dripping to the edge of the Peninsula and came to the block where he had left his clothes. There was now enough moon for him to see me.

"Richie?" he called.

I slept on, disgusted at having been a fool.

Max laughed gently and began to dress. In his coat he found cigarettes and lighter and began to smoke. The little flame, the smell of tobacco, made a distraction which I could recognize with dignity as a reason to wake up. I awoke.

"Hello," I said sleepily, sitting up.

"Hello. What time is it?"

"I don't know how long I've been sleeping."

"Were you concerned about me?"

"Asleep?"

"I see."

"Did you have a good swim?"

"Mostly under water. I wanted to see the view from Lethe. I've always believed an underground river ran below the quarry. The upper world would look quite different from there. The quarry is my entrance to the underworld. I went to be washed of my other life."

"And were you?"

"I won't know until I return to it again."

"Then you weren't, if it is still there."

"What are you so irritable about?"

"I hate to be waked up."

"I don't think you were really sleeping."

"You don't?"

"No, and I believe you were beginning to be worried when I stayed away so long, especially before the moon came up. You couldn't find the flashlight, could you."

"I didn't look for it."

"I put it in my shoe so I would be able to find it if I ever wanted to. You wouldn't think of looking there."

Unguardedly, I said,

"No, I didn't."

"So you did look."

"What of it."

"You were concerned for me," he asserted calmly.

Was it this he had gone to find out? How many suicides have been aborted by vanity, the curiosity of the self-victim to know the effect of his act? What pleasure remains in punishing someone if you don't know what you have made them feel? It was too much to admit, and moreover, it needed no further admission. He seemed content for the first time that night. To some degree, anyhow, he knew that I thought of him, and with concern. Our bickering annoyed me further, while it gave a small lift to his spirits. Suddenly again in his attitude of command, he said energetically,

"Let's go back. It must be late."

In silence I followed him up the ragged trail on the side of the ridge. He played his flashlight about with bravado, as if its beam were a rapier. Our return was so much less spectacular than the one I had agonized over in the dark by the quarry lake that I preserved my silence as a measure of dignity and reproof. What could I say to him? I could hardly say that I was glad he had returned safely without confessing below the words that I had thought of the alternative; and no more could I reproach him for not drowning without admitting that I regretted the loss of the sensational consequences which would have followed. Max, too, said little, only remarking as we drove up toward Newstead,

"Richie, I'm beginning to think you are a very complicated individual."

Nor could I protest this without claiming to be simple, and, so, not very interesting.

As we approached the Crystal Palace we saw that its grand illuminations were turned off. A few figures moved here and there in the limited light of ordinary work. The staff were restoring order after the party. Everyone else had gone.

So we must after all have been at the quarry for a matter of hours—two or more? The moon was high above the horizon. Its washy light made the countryside insubstantial, and the mists of long after midnight muffled the night creatures in their secret lodgments.

Running on to Newstead, we saw the house dark but for the main portico and lobby. No one was there—or so we

thought until we came in. Max's mother was waiting in a
huge brocaded armchair near the foot of the stair. When she
saw us she rose and we went to her. She had put off her red,
white, and blue jewels and had folded about herself a
dressing gown as plain as a linen sheet. She wore a ravaged
look, and now that she saw that her son was home, whatever
effort of self-supporting control she had kept up in her vigil
fell away, and cradling her carved hand she seemed to
diminish in her bones and sway on her feet. Max moved to
steady her but she nodded him away imperiously. We stood
before her. She turned to go upstairs, but paused facing me.
She looked into my face—to read what? I did not know. But
so intense was her look that I was aware only of her eyes—
dark coals of burning spirit in the long, blank oval of her
face. The anguish and energy of her wondering, all gathered
in her gaze, made the powdered skin about her eyes tremble
uncontrollably. Max lounged nearby, but she did not look at
him. She seemed to indicate that anyone who could abandon
his social duty and be rude to a hundred guests, not to
mention his parents and his all but fiancée, need not detain
the interest of any responsible person. But as for me: who
but myself could be interrogated with justice about the
matter? Who else had been asked to assume a splendid
responsibility? Who else had betrayed it either through
compliance or—worse—inspiration? If I was to blame, I
must be made to feel blameworthy. Where had he taken
me—or I him? Why? Was this what trust came to, always?
I could read such notions in her regard, and I felt a spurt of
anger at my bondage and the injustice which accompanied
the views of the rich. I made to speak, but she closed her eyes
in tragic patience, silencing me by her choice of misery.
Then disentangling her closed gaze from its mesh of lashes,

she looked long into my—I think this was the word she would have me use—my conscience; then she turned and with infinite weariness made her way upstairs.

❧ ❧ ❧

When I closed my eyes in the dark of my room I still saw the eyes of my cousin Alicia trembling in formless pale light. What made her wonder so, and look so into my heart, to discover what I knew of her son? Why had we vanished during such an important family festival? What had we fled from, what had we fled to? With what faith—broken or reaffirmed—did we return? Had we seen death? Life? Love? Despair? Futility? I could only dissolve her remembered gaze by opening my eyes and when I did so, I was once again the creature of a hostile summer.

The hum of summer was like the fever in my ears and in my bones which summoned me to manhood. Awake and mighty with desire I felt the hot meadows beyond my open window. Their scent, moving heavily on the slowly stirring air, smelled of generation—sap, crushed vegetable pungency, cast seed, snowy bark, dried sea foam, the ozone of wet minerals, the salt of tears and kisses. I begged of the dark to be let go, or granted consummation. The little motors of crickets sounding away in the multitudinous summer night seemed to eat mindlessly into the edges of my conscious mind. To resist such an invasion I must summon thought, any thought, and I remembered that country where I was the ruler, which I entered whenever I took a book to read.

Our house at home (the night began to lift its pressure as I thought of this) was full of the dark red leather volumes of Everyman's Library. My father would often come home with a package of five or six of the volumes and let me unwrap them. They had intricate gold designs on the spines in the manner of the Pre-Raphaelites, vines and leaves intertwined, and it was usually I who had first claim on the new volumes. I was not permitted to take them to my room on the top floor unless I could state that my schoolwork was all done; but if it was, there was no limit to the time I could spend with Everyman's. —I now was able to shut my eyes with safety, and instead of the stinging night, or Alicia's anguished wondering, I saw the backbones of our books, and I told over all the titles I could remember. I remembered a little scene of one time when my father had brought us some new books of the series, which lay rich and unsullied on the table in the living room. My mother took up one of the volumes and with a gaiety which abandoned her to a piece of drama in the presence of her husband and her son, while my father stood smiling at her with his arm around me, she read aloud in a lovely pealing tone of intimate belief in life's good things, so that we all had the same heady feeling: "Everyman, I will go with thee, and be thy guide, In thy most need to go by thy side"—the motto printed on the flyleaf of all the volumes, of which we had so many. In this modest cultural possession, which stood for more than itself, we all felt learned and lucky, valorous and faithful.

All the next day Newstead was silent. During the morning a message was brought to me that Mr Dana, the librarian, would like to see me in the library.

"The secretary thought we should give you this, although it is addressed to Mrs Chittenden. She is resting, so is Mr Chittenden, and Max is out of the house."

He handed me a telegram. It was sent by my father, granting permission for me to remain at Newstead for as long as pleased my cousins, provided I would be home for a week before schooltime, and provided further that all arrangements to remunerate me for my presence be dropped. My mother would send by express various articles of clothing and other things I might need for an extended stay.

"Thank you," I said to Mr Dana.

"It will be nice: to have you with us," he said. "Please use the library as much as you like. Max often spends hours here."

"Is he interested in Byron?"

"Ah: yes: the collection is the only thing at Newstead which appeals to him. But he reads everything else, too. We get the new books mainly for his sake. He likes to give me lists. A game—I make my own list of the new books, and when he brings his, we check them against each other to see how well I have guessed what he would like."

"Do you make a good score?"

"Quite: he is quite a remarkable young man. We often wonder what he—" He paused with the tact of a gentleman and the discretion of an employee.

"Wonder what?"

"My wife and I are extremely fond of him, he comes to

supper with us now and then, he adores our children, and we wonder what he will really do with himself. We can see how hard it is for someone in his special sort of position to decide what really interests him, and what he will spend his life at."

"He won't go into the Chittenden business, I suppose."

"Never. The last thing. He reads a great deal of science, but the big questions, he says, are not matters of fact but of feeling. Lately he has been reading miles of poetry. One day not long ago I asked him something, and he laughed and said he had been wanting to ask me what I thought of the same thing."

"What was it?"

"I asked him why he didn't make teaching his profession—studies of literature, chiefly poetry. And he said he had already been thinking of that. I think he would make a wonderful teacher. And you know?—it is one of the only things that an impossibly rich man can have as a vocation without seeming to have bought his way, or else remain an amateur."

"What do they think at Harvard?"

"His marks have suddenly improved almost out of sight. Next year, his last, should be his most brilliant; and of course: I think he ought to go right on and take his master's and doctor's degrees without interval; and then go to teach somewhere. —What do you think?"

He looked at me rather sidelong, from behind his thick dark-rimmed glasses. He was small, neat, gently spoken, and hungry for a little touch of the world beyond Chittenden Hills, and even I, a prep school senior, could bring him something that he, as a doctor of philosophy, a recognized expert on Byron, and the father of two young children

[151]

with another expected in a few weeks, could find interesting. But possibly he was asking me without words what I really thought of the prospects of any future for Maximilian. He was not sure of just the degree to which I might be considered "family" at Newstead, and so he invited my comment by hints and glances rather than by frank exposure of the clear thoughts behind his large lenses and alert black eyes. He was the same Andrew Dana who ten or twelve years later began to publish a series of successful stylishly "intellectual" novels which belonged to the end rather than to the beginning of a tradition, and so never had much influence or any imitators. But his dart of mind and charm of manner were in his pages, and reading them long afterward in their seasons I could hear his well-bred voice, and the comic accents with which he invested serious affairs, as if I, his early audience at Newstead, and the large public which rewarded him later, were all at about the same superior schoolboy level. He made up for being a man small in stature by taking cheeky risks now and then in what he might say, and at such moments he invited forgiveness in advance by the candid self-mockery of his smile, while rocking from side to side on his excellent English brogans.

He seemed always to be watching himself, and speaking for his own pleasure. There was something of all this manner in his books. The best known of these was a set of three novels which he called *Ruins by Moonlight: A Gothic Trilogy,* and its separate volumes reflected well enough what he knew about Newstead: Volume One, *The Abbey,* Volume Two, *The Heir,* and Volume Three, *The Quarry.* He published also a speculative biography called *In Search of Lord Clare,* about the friend of Byron's long-cherished youthhood passion.

"I think Max would be a fine teacher," I said. "He always seems to go direct to what interests him. Students would like that. He could make things seem simple."

"Ah. But do you think him simple?"

"Oh, no, not himself. —And he doesn't think anybody else is, either. He told me yesterday that I was complicated."

"And aren't you?"

"I never thought about it. I don't think I am."

"Do you ever have dreams?"

"Oh yes."

"And do they seem at odds with your waking world?"

"Often."

"And isn't that complicated?"

"I suppose so. —But the dreams don't really seem like me. I have no control over them."

"Ah. Ah. My dear fellow: perhaps I should not inform you: but we are everything that happens to us, including those things we cannot control. Once you know that, you cease to be simple. And knowing so is to pass a certain stage of life irreversibly and forever. It is a *kind* of loss of a *kind* of virginity—" with a gleam on the last word which must have caused any prep school class to break into rowdy laughter. I laughed.

"The Family are invisible today," he said. "Would you lunch with me here?" He was desperate to have anyone to talk to, even a sixth-former.

"Thank you."

He used the house phone on his desk and told the pantry that there would be two for luncheon in the round conservatory. Then,

"Yes," he resumed, "the trouble is: if it is a trouble: that once you are aware that everything is complicated, you never can get away from it. Anything that you once saw as simple seems like a reproach and a mystery once you are taken beyond it. It ought to be quite the other way round. But there it is."

"But many people never even think about it."

"Or anything, of course. —But others, like Max, for example, see all aspects of everything at once, and if you do that, how do you know which one is the one that belongs truly to you? Is it luck? It may just be luck. Perhaps it all depends on how lucky—that is, how creative instead of destructive—our early dreams are. Perhaps they establish for us in our youth the principle of our choices in the world. But yes: oh heavens yes: they must be true dreams, that is, they must come to us unconsciously, and only later have some meaning. Otherwise there is real danger in what they might do to us."

"I don't think I understand."

"Ah: I am clumsy: I mean of course that if dreams cease to be unconscious, and begin to be asked for consciously, or if they come from events we have known consciously which have the power of nightmare, then: then: something about them sets us in their light forever, perhaps." He looked at me with his signal of daring, the smile which said he was going to step beyond the station to which the munificence of Alexander Chittenden had summoned him, and said (to a member of the family!), "I have wondered if Max's at times unsettling behavior might result from confusions once known face to face but long forgotten in the upper mind while they continue to propose denials and defiances in the lower."

We were called to the conservatory. On our way out of the great dusky room we came to a heavy and highly polished

Renaissance table on which a single object rested. From a pinpoint aperture in the center of a gilded rosette in the coffered ceiling high above came a narrow cone of light which cast an island of soft glow upon the center of the table; and in it rested a bronze sculpture of Leda and the Swan. Mr Dana paused and looked upon it.

"It could hardly be more explicit, do you think?" he said invitingly.

And yes, it was a bronze enactment, in the most passionate elegance, of the union of Leda and Zeus the almighty father. I remembered the story from my schoolbook of Gayley's *Classic Myths,* but I never thought to see so intimately that godly embrace enfolding the queenly body whose head lay back in wonder while her eyes gazed out of sight in ecstasy at the divine invisible. Classical rapes in art always made me thoughtful in the youthful days of my awakened but unsatisfied desire, and in museums I gave my attention less to mythology than to anatomy. Now I could not help the bent of my thought toward a perhaps unworthy but quite practical question. How did the swan actually manage what he was about? A breathing quilt of white feathers? A secret portal of pulsing smooth flesh? What possible union? But then I remembered of course that since he was a god, explanations were beside the point. The statue was perhaps fourteen inches high. I wanted to touch it but refrained.

"Jacopo Sansovino," said Mr Dana. "1486–1570. We sent photographs to Mr Berenson. We have two letters from him here. In the first he gave it firmly to Jacopo, and Mist' Chittenden was delighted. Then came the second in which B.B. said that on further study of the photographs, he would have to say 'Follower Of.' Consternation. We then had Duveen down to look at it, and he didn't hesitate. He said he would be proud to acquire it as a Sansovino for Mr Frick at twice what Mist' Chittenden paid for it, whatever that might be. Relief and joy. But of course there was no idea of letting it go. —The Metropolitan has since asked for it, too."

We were supposed to be going in to lunch, but Mr Dana was held by the Leda, though he saw it a hundred times a day. He put his hand on it and reminiscently traced the serpentine curve of the swan's neck.

"Yes," he said in daydream; and then grew brisk and professional in a librarianly way. "Yes, this: it has just come from Chatto and Windus." He held up an almost square slim volume of poetry called *Leda*. "By Huxley's grandson," he said. "Listen to this—" and he read from the poem in a voice which at first he caused to bleat artificially as if to strike me with the power of poetry as a universal classroom instrument:

> *"Closer he nestled, mingling with the slim*
> *Austerity of virginal flank and limb*
> *His curved and florid beauty, till she felt*
> *That downy warmth strike through her flesh and melt*
> *The bones and marrow of her strength away.*
> *One lifted arm bent o'er her brow, she lay*
> *With limbs relaxed, scarce breathing, deathly still,*
> *Save when a quick, involuntary thrill*
> *Shook her sometimes with passing shudderings,*
> *As though some hand had plucked the aching strings*
> *Of life itself, tense with expectancy.*
> *And over her the swan shook slowly free*
> *The folded glory of his wings, and made*
> *A white-walled tent of soft and luminous shade*
> *To be her veil and keep her from the shame*
> *Of naked light and the sun's noonday flame."*

[156]

Losing its make-believe, his voice went dry and he looked aside with a truly suffering glance at another world, and the sting of tears seemed to sound in his voice when he resumed and finished the poem:

> *"Hushed lay the earth and the wide, careless sky.*
> *Then one sharp sound, that might have been a cry*
> *Of utmost pleasure or of utmost pain,*
> *Broke sobbing forth, and all was still again."*

He softly shut the book and with bent head restored it to the rack of current publications. He blinked his eyes free of the Attic skies, and said,

"Yes, we must go to lunch," and again began to lead me from the library. But after a few rocking steps he paused and began to laugh.

"But the best part: perhaps you haven't heard the best part of our Leda story—unless Mist' Chittenden told it to you yesterday?"

I shook my head.

"Oh, really priceless," said Mr Dana. "About the new housekeeper and Leda?"

"No, really," I said.

"Well, if Mist' Chittenden does tell it to you, you must pretend not to have heard it before. It always makes him laugh to tell it."

I promised.

"Yes: well: a while ago we engaged a new housekeeper, and Miss Magruder was showing her around the place. They came in here, and the housekeeper—she was a bony old thing got up in black alpaca—ran her finger along the table looking for dust, and suddenly she saw the Leda there in the

[157]

center. She stopped and gasped, and said to Miss Magruder, 'My stars! *what's that duck up to!'*"

We both laughed, and this time we really marched on to the conservatory where lunch was waiting.

"I might add that the housekeeper did not last here very long. Somehow not quite our tone, don't you know. —But I have reflected on the episode many times, in relation to the optimistic belief that great art sanctions any subject matter. You know?"

I said I did, and then as we took our places amidst the greenery which gleamed with fine drops of spray recently syringed over the tropical leaves, I asked,

"Where do you suppose Max is?"

"He didn't tell you?"

"No."

"Nor me. I don't know. His man simply said he'd gone out early leaving a note saying he wouldn't be back for lunch."

"Do you suppose he went to the quarry?"

"I don't know. —Have you been there with him?"

"Yes. Yesterday afternoon, and then again last night."

"Oh. Ah. So that's where you went last night. I rather thought as much. —He always goes there when those times overtake him."

"Times?"

"Or you might prefer to say moods. But moods is a trivial word for what comes to him. —The quarry seems to have almost a mystical fascination for him. How often I have seen him go past our little place to the ridge and up the road and over. In winter vacations when the quarry is frozen he goes there to skate, and in summer, to swim, and sometimes for a whole day he will go there with books and come back after dark."

"He said the quarry is his entrance to the underworld."

Mr Dana put down his knife and fork and gazed at me.

"Ah: yes: ah: you see? As I said? It is that sort of conscious dream I meant. Do you see? Is it—can anything be—truly a legend if one makes it deliberately?"

I shook my head. I did not understand.

I remembered later that all during lunch, whenever I handed Mr Dana something he could not reach at the table, he did not take it direct from me, but waited fastidiously until I had set it down and taken my hand away; only then would he take it up in turn.

※ ※ ※

It was a day of messages. Late in the afternoon Marietta telephoned to me to say that Max was with her, they were getting things together right now, we three were going to the quarry for a picnic supper, with nobody else along. We were going to swim and drink beer (excellent Canadian beer purveyed to Max by his bootlegger) and think up things to do for the rest of the summer now that it was known that I was to remain until late August. They would come for me within the hour. Dress sloppy, Max said, and bring a large towel. We would stop for Chief and he would swim with us. Max wanted the concertina from his cluttered sitting room—would I please look for it and have it with me at the rear terrace when they called for me? He did not want to come into the house for fear of getting involved.

[159]

Presently there was another telephone call. Miss Magruder, the secretary, whom I never saw, was asked by Mrs Chittenden to say that Mr Standish had telephoned from the greenhouses with an alert about the night-blooming cereus—it was certain to open tonight, and, in his opinion, during the late evening, if the twilight were overcast. Mrs Chittenden wanted the household to gather for dinner on the terrace at the Crystal Palace so as to be readily at hand when the flower began to move. Cars would be waiting at a quarter before seven to take us down the hill. Mr Chittenden was resting and did not plan to come, but Mrs Chittenden expected everyone else, including the Danas, as Mr Dana would be "taking notes." Mr Maximilian, she hoped, would take photographs. Could Miss Magruder tell Mrs Chittenden that I would be there?

I explained about the picnic.

In that case, she would telephone to Miss Osborne at once and ask her to rearrange her picnic plans, for Mrs Chittenden of course wanted her also to be with us, as well as Mr Maximilian.

Should I wait to know what to do?

No, thought Miss Magruder, I could assume that the picnic was canceled, as Mrs Chittenden particularly wanted everyone with her at a moment which meant so much to her.

—So much to her who had so little else to excite her interest or happiness, I knew, and I knew that the event of the cereus held more than merely the tyranny of a hobby. During how many hours had my cousin Alicia thought about the slow gathering of forces within the impassive cactus plant, and wondered when it would come in flower, and whether she would be present to see it, and if anyone

[160]

else might possibly realize what it would mean to her to see it? In her helplessness she, who no longer made acts of charm and objects of beauty with her hands, had faithfully given of what she possessed—her interest, money, and time —to assure the *cereus grandiflora* the fulfillment of its cycle. Surely those who loved her and whom she loved would of their own hearts wish to be with her tonight?

But it was too much to hope for from Max. My telephone rang again and he spoke to me.

"Forget this commotion about the Crystal Palace tonight. I told my mother's secretary we would not come. She said you already told her about the picnic. The picnic still holds."

"No," said Marietta, taking the phone from him, "I told Max and I tell you we must; Richard, we must go with Aunty Lissy. Just tonight. It wouldn't matter any other time. But we are going to be with her if she wants us, and she does."

"I think we should, too," I said.

"You see?" she said to Max behind her, "you can't have a picnic alone. Let's just have ours tomorrow night, and tonight we'll—"

There was a stormy mutter off-phone, and Marietta relayed it to me.

"He says he hates to have anyone change his plans for him. Oh, yes, and so do I. But tonight is different.—What?" she asked turning her sound away from the phone and listening to Max beyond her somewhere. Then, "All right, I'll tell him," she said, facing her words toward me over the phone again. "Max says we have to have this picnic for a special reason."

"What special reason?" I asked.

She turned and repeated my question and came back with an answer.

"He says he has to get back something he gave you."

"Gave me?" I said. "He didn't give me anything."

Pause, inquiry, return, while my mind's eye watched them in their exchanges.

"Yes he did,'" she reported, "he says he did. He says it was an idea of himself that he gave you, and he says he has to get it back, and give you another."

I was exasperated by this complicated exchange, with its suggestion of negotiations through a neutral party, and yet I was also ready to laugh at it. An idea of himself? I frowned trying to remember, but could not. All I could think of was his concern of this moment, and that seemed very like him.

"What?" asked Marietta, turning to Max again. "Oh. Of course. Why not. —Richie, he says we'll go to see the damned cactus perform, if we are all being so dull about it; but he says we'll go to the quarry anyway, afterward. He says we should probably stay all night on the Peninsula, without telling anyone, the three of us. Would you like that?"

"Oh, yes."

At the suggestion, and its formless promises, a little spray of desire seemed to go throughout me, along my nerves. I laughed, and at how I sounded, Marietta laughed, too, in an involuntary betrayal of unexpected excitement, as if I had suddenly forced her breath by laying my head below her breasts and pressing it hungrily upon her soft belly. She broke the spell by turning again to Max.

"What?"

But Max had come closer and I heard his own voice.

"Tell him that there are only three creatures I love on this earth—my girl, my cousin, and my dog. Don't you ever leave me, any of you." He was, then, sure of no one. Solitude beckoned.

ꕤ ꕤ ꕤ

In Max's bearing, that night as we dined on the terrace, I thought there was a hint that his perverse unkindness to his mother now represented an attitude he had established so firmly that he must sustain it for the sake of what was expected of him. It had the air almost of a protective convention—an eccentricity excused by its long-established habit, no matter where it came from. Marietta could work nervously to keep the peace between him and us all, and this would add to his importance as a trying creature to have around. It was an effect his mother enhanced by her pleading sweetness that night. In her longing desire to let nothing mar her great moment, she presented to Max and all of us a ravaged face that held a smile of forgiveness for her son's brutal rudeness, past, present, or future. The sentimental tug of this was great, and it gave her an advantage over Max which was almost intolerable. It seemed to him unfair, when so much in life was disgusting, to smile it away. If he could have defined his duty, he might have said that it was his duty to let nothing escape exposure and punishment which deserved it. If he were asked, "Under whose laws?" he would have answered, "My own."

There were places set for Mr and Mrs Dana but we sat down without them and the footmen began to serve us at once.

[163]

"I wonder what can have become of the Danas," murmured Aunt Lissy.

"I trust they had the wit to forgo this doubtful event," said Max. "Many people would not willingly squander a whole night waiting for a somniculous plant to bloom which comes in season only once in several years."

Aunt Lissy said to me, instead of replying to him,

"Jane Dana is to have a baby soon. Possibly something to do with that. They are so polite, I am sure there would be a reason for their not coming, or coming late."

"Mr Dana has learned in a hard school how to be polite," said Max. "We have a way here of collecting our dues."

"Yes, my dear," said his mother, and her fabricated hand actually made a small beginning of a loving gesture toward him, before it must halt and be restored by her other hand to a position less physically painful.

We were at a small round table in a pool of lantern light. Behind us the high glass wall of the Crystal Palace rose to its pinnacles and domes and slopes like an iceberg. The lights within, reflecting off the airy greenery under the vault, had a greenish-blue cast, and turned the air into a likeness of underwater distances.

I do not remember all that we talked about, only that Marietta, Aunt Lissy, and I kept up a semblance of conversation while Max limited himself to an occasional sardonic comment, at which Marietta would scream with comic reproof, while Aunt Lissy thanked her with luxuriant blinkings. My discomfort was great. It was not eased when at one point Aunt Lissy said to me,

"Richard, we are all so happy that you are now a member of our household. We are now *family* in the best sense, aren't we? We do so hope you will be happy with us. You must always feel quite independent with us, for that is how we all are with each other, aren't we?"

She rayed the table with a serenely confident glance. There was no response except a small rapturous groan of appreciation from Marietta. But I felt now that I had been sealed in my position as one of the Newstead staff, and to be warned to preserve my independence by the very one who had taken it away was chilling. Before I could comment, one of the servants came and leaned over me and said softly that I was wanted outside.

I looked at Aunt Lissy to be excused, and she nodded, too gracious to show surprise. I left the table and followed the manservant through great aisles of glass lined with tropical trees and plants to the driveway entrance of the Crystal Palace. There, moving his body, but not his feet, with perturbation, was Mr Dana.

❦ ❦ ❦

Without preamble, he said in a thin voice,
"Listen: he's dead!"
"Who?"
"I killed him. —But it could not be helped!"
I felt my face taking the wild look of his own as I tried to read his message. So fast does the mind work that before he spoke again I conceived a drama in which the librarian, out of years of envy and false respect, had murdered Alexander Chittenden in a book-lined bay of the library where even now the body lay at the edge of a spill of gold lamplight.
"Who, Mr Dana? Tell me plainly."

[165]

"I can't go in there and tell them," he said, pleading to be excused like a sick man, "you must do it for me. But don't tell them until I have left."

"You aren't staying?"

"Great God no."

He moved from side to side with distress. In the spill of greenish glow from the great conservatory he was haggard. With his chick haircut, he looked like a sick child. He had a motoring cap in his hands which he wrung. I had never before seen anybody actually wringing anything with agitation. He said that he and his wife Jane had left home out on the quarry road in good time to get here for dinner, and to see the cereus—he had his notebook and pencils in his pocket to describe the blooming as Mrs Chittenden had asked him to do. They drove along the road near Mr Standish's cottage and all of a sudden, when he could least have expected it, Maximilian's dog had leaped out from the hedges and attacked his left front tire, dancing and growling. His wife had screamed, "Look out, Tony!" and he had swerved the car to the right, toward the roadside ditch, but the dog pressed his attack, having a frolicking time, and then Jane cried out again that they were going to fall into the ditch and turn over, and she had half-tried to jump out, but he had grasped her and at the same time turned the car up on the road again. Chief had not expected this, but he leaped out of the way, or rather, tried to, but the car was jumping also, and as it regained the level road it had a spurt of speed, the front wheel threw the dog back under the car, and the rear wheel passed over him, and he was dead.

"Are you sure?" I asked, horrified at last.

"Oh yes. We stopped, my wife became almost hysterical, she made me get out to go and look. I have trouble with that sort of thing, I couldn't go closer, and I said we could see he was dead, but she insisted in being sure, if the dog should need help, and I had to go and look, and while I looked he heaved once or twice and then stopped. He died. It was too dreadful. You've no idea."

He was shaking with the recollection of it.

He had gone back to the car and his wife told him she could not possibly go on to dinner. She was faint and sick, and she too was trembling at what happened. She told him to pull the dog off the road on to the grass by the roadside, and then they would have to go home and telephone their regrets, and tell what had happened.

He looked at me sorrowfully. All his dancing literacy and authority had left him. He was a man in shame and trouble. He said that he had been unable to touch the dog to pull him away decently, he could not say why. As he now thought of doing it, his stomach heaved and he went into a sweat. His wife began to cry—she was afraid for her unborn baby, for the wrath of Newstead, for the loss of a good job just when expenses were going to increase, and for everything. He had to get her home. But first he went to the Standish house to tell someone what had happened and to ask them to take charge. No one came. Then he knew of course that Mr Standish was at the greenhouse, and his wife probably off visiting somewhere. He returned to his car and took his wife home. She nearly fainted when they got there. Then he turned around and came here to explain—but he found he was unable to face Max, or his mother, and so he had sent for me.

"Is the dog still there?" I asked, for my mind was still crowded with pictures of what had happened and how.

"Oh, yes: hideous: I was almost unable to drive past it.

[167]

What am I going to do? What am I going to do? —Will you tell them for me?"

"I don't know," I said, thinking not of his misery but of the already charged evening in the family. Aunt Lissy's lovely event, great to her, however trivial it might seem to anyone else, would be marred by this wretched story. Maximilian's state of mind already seemed desperate. Surely the thing to do was wait to bring any bad news until after the flowers had come. I told Mr Dana,

"If I tell them I will wait until this is over here."

"Yes, splendid": he said, ghastly in the eagerness of an indicated reprieve. "In that way they won't hear it until after I am gone. How revolting it all is!"

"Yes. But it was an accident."

"Yes, it was, wasn't it! Yes: how criminal of those people to let their dogs run loose. What can you expect! —Oh yes, another thing, though," he said, his eyes working in search of his thoughts, "you'll have to tell them *something* right away. —Tell them my wife has suddenly been taken ill, nothing serious, but she cannot come, and I cannot leave her, and thank Mrs Chittenden for me. Here": he thrust his notebook and pencils upon me. "Tell her I asked you to make the notes instead, as I have to go."

With a sudden dry sob he felt the urgency of having to go, and turned, and ran to his little car, and drove away.

I returned to the family and told how Jane Dana could not be left this evening, and we all sounded regretful; but Marietta hunched her thin active shoulders toward each other, and told me in silence that she knew there was something beyond this to detain me for so many minutes with Mr Dana. I felt my responsibility, and I frowned slightly to warn her to let things be. It was a heavy sky over us, darkening toward night. I thought of everything in black and white, and I saw the quarry road running straight away toward the lost ridge, and in the foreground, inert in a sprawl that would have looked playful if there had been any chance of recovery from it with a leaping gaiety, lay the smooth white body with its startling black spots.

"What?" and Marietta, leaning to read my face.

"Nothing."

※ ※ ※

We were lifting our coffee cups for a first sip—mine shook a little in my hand—when the butler came to lean over Mrs Chittenden to say,

"Mr Standish thinks you had better come without delay, madam."

She put her hand to her cheek like a girl and came lightly to stand.

"Oh, how beautiful," she exclaimed, as if she could already see the flower. "Max, darling, hurry, fetch your camera from the car."

"I didn't bring it."

"Ah, Max. Ah, dearest, why could you not— No matter. Let's hurry."

She took my arm. We went into the Crystal Palace and made our way to the far bay of glass where alone on its earth bench stood the wooden tub with its five uprearing stalks of prickly glazed green. Mr Standish was waiting.

"Oh, Mr Standish—"

"Yes, ma'am. You can already see just the littlest lightening of color in the nearest bud."

We crowded to the bench. Each of the thick upright stalks supported a slender stem of dove-gray about two inches long, at the end of which was a folded bud of succulent green, perhaps as large as a pecan nut. The sleeping petals were folded tight in each bud, but in the one nearest to us the first faint movement had already begun, and though we did not yet see movement, we could see how a fissure between petals was made plain by the revelation of a paler green than that of the outer shells. Mr Standish, not daring to train lights on the plant, even so had set up a movie camera on a tripod, in the hope of recording what we had all come to see. Aunt Lissy said,

"How thoughtful and kind of you, Mr Standish, to arrange for the filming. We forgot to bring our camera."

I saw Marietta press Max's arm, to prevent any relentless restatement of this.

"Oh, look, my darlings," said Aunt Lissy, leaning forward. Mr Standish released the camera trigger.

The nearest bud showed us a tiny quake as the sticky edges of its petals tried to separate from the form which had held them in obscurity for months. The pale fissure widened ever so slightly, but we could detect the difference.

"And look!"

A higher stalk behind the near one gave its hidden, fiercely defended power to its bud, and that too made a miniature tremor in the air and declared its life.

There was something awesome and painful in seeing the act of blind fulfillment so faithfully enacted even in so small a scale. How much of my feeling was induced by the emotion so tensely suspended all about us in the air I do not know. But the blind flowers reaching for light, and the longing of my Aunt Lissy to have a part in this act of life, and the brooding resentfulness of Max playing about the great purity of the event, and my own susceptibility to charged atmospheres—all made my heart beat and my mouth dry up.

Mr Standish shut down the camera.

"It will be slow," he said, explaining why he must be thrifty with his available film.

Aunt Lissy held my arm and I could feel her quivering with concentration which I mistook for fatigue. Mr Standish offered to bring her a chair. She thanked him and refused. There would be time for exhaustion later, later, but for now, she knew only a time for passion, even if it was a passion which we bestowed on the flowering which in itself, so far as we could know, had no feeling.

How unbearable a certain kind of silence could be to those who had no peace within. The minutes, the quarter hours ticked by, and we stood and watched while nothing further happened. We could hear each other's breathing, the remote rustle or creak of cloth or leather as we moved to find relief after holding one position. Now and then I thought I heard rain, or a fountain, but I could not be sure it was not the hiss of my own pulse in my ears. Some of the air vanes were open in the upper vault of the Crystal Palace and in our stillness we could hear the passage of air making a soft leathery clatter in the highest leaves of the banana palms which stood along the tallest aisle. I watched the cereus so intently that I would see movement where there was none until, after what seemed an endless and unnerving time of attention, Aunt Lissy glanced sharply at Mr Standish, who nodded, agreeing that it had begun again, and we all gazed with our various love or scorn at the awakening buds.

It was like a strange earthbound astronomy—so slowly, yet now so continuously did the flowers, all of them, begin to move. As you can measure the passage of stars best by glancing away and then returning to see them in new positions, so from now until the end we could measure the actual opening of the *cereus grandiflora* best by resting our eyes, looking away into the misty green of the aisles, and then returning to watch again; and each time as we did so we could see each flower more open to the air than when we had last looked.

For after the first struggle of each bud to free itself of the confining form of long sleep, the flowers began to declare themselves not only free of restraint but of darkness. They unfurled what seemed to be shafts of light. The flowers were going to be pure white, with petals rather like those of a ragged daisy. Their white as it was revealed with infinite slowness seemed to release radiance. To see them giving off light as they unfolded their fresh delicate fabric was to see a mystery solved at last; and to feel a sense of life's blessing.

The smallest change in the size, position, or tint of the flowers became a large event. So it was when the nearest flower reached the point of opening at which we could see that its center was a soft golden yellow, the color of bees, in the shape of a small mounded cushion.

"How adorably exquisite," exclaimed Aunt Lissy on an indrawn whisper, as if she were fearful of disturbing the continuing fulfillment with a breath or a word. Above the rich green of the stalks, with their protective sheath of fine needles outlining their fibrous living strength, at last the white flowers with their golden centers stood fully open.

"Oh, how to thank!" whispered Aunt Lissy.

She herself felt like the cereus opening, in a transference of life. The white pure light of the petals seemed to open in order to free her of sorrow and loss in her own life, and as she joined the life of the flowers, her radiance was rapt and beautiful, if painful, to behold. I saw the face my mother remembered with so much lasting youthful love. She was forgetful of all but what reached into the dense air before her.

The mystery unfolding had held us all so that we had lost awareness of each other; but now I happened to glance at my Cousin Max, and I saw him watching not the passion of the flower but his mother's. As I watched him, his face clouded over and I thought I saw in it the love which he refused her. For a moment his ambiguous eyes under their classically chiseled brows shone with tears; but the heat of his feeling dried them up, and he looked away. He puckered his lips in silent whistling, like a small boy watching the empty distance as if idly unconcerned.

The cereus, opening, existed to achieve what no one there could do—to bloom into fulfillment without let or thought, and in opening to full life, neither give nor feel pain. No wonder, I think now, that Max, so quick to see the opposite face of the obvious, could not bear it.

The flowers were so white that all near things seemed to be revealed by them. We had abandoned our scale of time and adopted that of the secret calendar of growth and delivery deep in the shafts of the plant. It was difficult to return to our own sense of time measured. How to withdraw from a sacrament?

Max felt his obligation to manage this for us. In a light, clear voice, he said,

"The event has simple material implications, too. For example, it would be amusing to know how much it has cost in money to bring this one hideous, prickly vegetable to its climax tonight."

"Max, hush, please, dear," said his mother. "Let us simply enjoy it."

"Yes, but once it is over, an orgasm—even such a stately one as this tonight—means little."

Mr Standish had stopped his camera, and now he began to fold it away. He was offended by Max's tone.

"I believe that it is all finished, ma'am," he said.

Aunt Lissy nodded wearily.

"Yes. I suppose so. But I believe I shall wait a little while and just look at the blossoms. I can see just how to paint them."

"Yes, then," said Max, "we will run along. —You will be taken home?"

"Yes, there will be a car. Good night, children?" Her inflection asked us a question of loving care—where would we go? What would we do? But no one replied.

We thanked her and guiltily began our escape. I remembered that I had meant to take notes, but had neglected to do so, but thought it didn't matter, as I would never forget anything of that evening. Aunt Lissy suddenly made a wild little cry, as if shaken by a premonition of sin or death. She called after us,

"Max, please come here a minute!"

He stopped, motioned us to go on, and returned to his mother. Marietta and I walked down the aisle and then paused to wait for him. He went to his mother, and I saw her raise her face and look long into his. She spoke to him. He stood motionless. We could not hear what she was saying, or what he answered in a moment. Marietta said to me urgently,

"What was all that at dinner? You looked so odd when you returned."

I told her.

"Oh, no, no!" she exclaimed. She crossed her arms and clutched her shoulders as if to protect herself from blows. "What are we going to do? I have had the saddest time all day with him—Richie, I am really afraid for the first time."

"Of him?"

"Yes, and more than that, for him."

"What did he do?"

"Not what he did. But oh, how he sounded. My father is worried about him. God knows what he might do. —The quarry, last night, you know?"

I nodded.

"He told me he wished he had never come back."

I remembered the thought I had tried to resist all that night at the quarry.

"Help him, Richie. I have tried. I am useless."

"Perhaps everyone is."

"We must never think that, if we love him."

"Do you love him?"

"Yes. I ought to leave him but I can't. Do you?"

"I don't know. It is soon. And he won't let me or anyone."

"He loves you."

"He doesn't show it."

"Oh, yes he does, if you read backwards everything he says and does. —He doesn't need a long time to know if he loves somebody or not."

"Why does he hate his mother so?"

"Oh, Richie, he doesn't, doesn't. I just told you:"

[175]

How young we were, and trying how hard, to bring into the common light the shadowy troubles that beset Max— and all youth, to one degree or another. We turned to see him then. His mother set her hand upon his cheek. He shook his head. He held his arms out from his sides as if to forbid them. And then, almost as slowly as the unfolding of the cereus flowers, he brought his arms to embrace her, he bent to her, and kissed her, and even from our distance, we felt the aching bewilderment of his demand and denial, and the balm of that kiss. We never knew what she said to him to bring him to her for that moment; but the sight of their peace together is what I see most plainly when I think of anything that happened that night.

"He is coming now, Richard—what shall we tell him?"

"You tell him."

"No, you!"

"No, he will take it better from you."

He joined us and we went quickly outside. He moved abruptly, with airs of command which silenced us. Strange currents of feeling were adrift in the castle, cold winds blew compellingly through the prince's thoughts, he desired his people to be silent while he asked questions of the future which could not be answered.

I felt like my younger self at the time when I read our Everyman Shakespeare—the last act of *Othello,* with troubled wonderings which seemed to call toward them in fateful answer those events which were no less powerful for being imagined.

Once outside we came to Max's car which shone with rich dim lights in the glow reflected from the Crystal Palace. There his racing thoughts seemed to slow their pace. He turned and leaned against the side of the car facing the glass walls. He smiled with unarranged sweetness. He said,

"Richie?"

"Yes."

"Come here."

He took my shoulders in his grinding grip and shook me not in anger but in longing to know what he now asked, while Marietta, excluded from the mystery, looked at us in turn, back and forth, back and forth.

"Richie, why did you pretend to be sleeping? That was the worst thing."

"You mean last night at the quarry?"

"Yes."

I was humilated at any reference to my foolish games of the imagination the night before. I replied coldly,

"Why do you care?"

It was a question I have wished I had never asked. The effect of it was to make my cousin, that imperious, self-regarding youth who ravened splendidly after life without knowing what he sought—the effect of it was to make him diminish in spirit until he was forlorn—or, better said in the language my mother spoke from her German-American girlhood, *verloren*. Lost? He? He dropped his hands from me and his lips parted ruefully. In the just sufficient glow from the Crystal Palace I saw what came to him in answer to my heartless question. He suddenly looked old and ravished, betraying his likeness to his mother and his father. If I ever loved him it was then—and too late. I saw that I had committed him to suffer—just how, I did not then know; but a surge of feeling made me want to repair what I had done. I put my hand toward him, and said,

"Max! I mean, I don't know what to say!"

"You have said it," he answered, and then he inflated his chest and assumed his public presence—solicitous, impersonal, and charming. "Let's go," he said, with all the courtesy of despair.

We entered the car.

"Max, where are we going?" asked Marietta.

"As we said. To the quarry."

"Max, something," she said in a voice made light by fear.

"Yes?"—driving with a sweep down to the quarry road.

"Do you remember when Dana came at dinnertime?"

"Of course."

"He has done something dreadful."

"I've always expected that he would."

"Richie, tell him."

"Are you both afraid to tell me?"

"Yes. —Richie, tell him."

I told him. He slowed the car as he heard but did not come to a stop. When all the details of how Chief had been killed and where he lay now were told, Max said nothing. He took up speed again. We looked at his profile in the faint light from the instrument dials. He was scowling deeply over a smile which gave a musing sweetness to his mouth. We burrowed into the dark heavy air with our headlamp beams. The shafted light bobbled above the wavery macadam road and Marietta was the first to see what it revealed in our lancing thrusts ahead. There on the road lay a white object with startling black spots marking its sprawled form. The car gained speed, and I thought that it must have done so through some independent power of its own. The sprawl grew larger directly in our path. We must turn aside, and decelerate, and stop.

"Max!" cried Marietta. "Don't you see him?"

A new thrust of speed answered her. We were aiming
directly for the dead body of the dog.

"Max! Look out, you fool!"

There was a certain bulk to the volume taken up by a full-
grown Dalmatian hound. Even the long, heavy frame of the
Isotta-Fraschini must reflect a rubbery impact with such an
object. The front wheels held but the rear wheels danced
aside in a small skid, quickly recovered, reflecting the action
of passing solidly, with tumbling disturbance, over the obstacle which lay in the roadway. We could feel in our own
contained, moist, living flesh the trundled deformation of
that inert mass on the surfaced road in the dark beneath us.
One, two, and we had passed—but not before we knew what
destruction in break, evisceration, crush of bone, and spurt
of fluid we had done. Max drove on and we dared not look
at him, but Marietta, leaning forward and crushing her
hands upon her face, screamed,

"Stop, stop, I must get out!"

I was still thrown about in my bones by the abandoned
form my cousin had violated. Marietta cried again,

"Make him stop!"

She pulled at me, drawing blood with her nails, and I
shouted,

"Max, stop! Let her out!"

In a hundred yards or so he began to slow down, and in
another hundred, the car came to rest. Marietta, holding her
hand across her face, threw herself past me into the roadside
and ran away into the brushy shadows to the rear. Max sat
still gazing without expression into the darkness ahead.

"Good God," I said. "What did you do that for!"

There was no answer, or so I thought; but held aloft by
the instrument lights his profile against the darkness had a

dreamy detachment of expression which in its way was sufficient answer, when I saw it.

"Listen," I said vehemently, "one of us ought to go after her!"

"No, don't," he said. "She will come back. She always has."

I was immobilized by his unconcern, until I saw it as another aspect of the despair which had brought us to this moment. Then I was driven away by desire to disbelieve what had happened.

"I am going to her!" I shouted, and I vaulted out of the car and ran back into the darkness where Marietta had fled. The car remained still, its lights flooding ahead, its controlling intelligence captive to the dark of its own nature.

※ ※ ※

She was kneeling in the undergrowth by the side of the road. When I spoke to her she answered me with a breath and sank down lower. I bent to touch her and found her hands, which she held upon her head, drawing it down, down, into darkness darker and friendlier than the night. She was shaking helplessly. I lifted her into my arms and she lay upon my breast covering her face with her hands. Everything was still except night sounds in the meadow.

"Hush," I said to her, speaking to the outcries in her thought. She shook her head, then she shuddered away from me to look up at my face as if she could see it and she said in a caught whisper,

"He doesn't know how he is!"

It was a discovery which she had never thought to make. Through years and days it had all been a game, in which she was Max's creature, doing whatever he asked, and always thinking that so long as everyone understood that it was only a game, nothing harmful was in it. But now she knew, and the knowledge did not release her. She said,

"But now more than ever I cannot leave him."

"I don't see why not."

"No, you don't see." She took her hands from her face and put them to mine. She said, "Richie, don't leave us!" At the idea of being abandoned, she began to cry. She scolded herself for this, and presently added, "But I am sure we are all too much for you."

"We'll see."

"But you know something?" She was trying to return to the local habit of prattle about serious affairs. "One thing I can never believe: I can never believe that beauty can hold danger, or evil."

I have thought about this since, but at the time, I was put off by it, and a distraction came out of the meadow air, and I turned to listen. It was the whistle of the down-bound freight, coming along the level roadbed at the base of the ridge. It made me think of going: we could not stay in the roadside bramble all night.

"Marietta," I said, "let's go back, now, we'll get Max to take us home."

She nodded against me and we stood up. I held the low branches aside for her as we stepped out to the road. We saw the car bulked against its headlights, and as we looked, the car began to move away from us. In the grind and growl of its sudden furious acceleration, we heard nothing else, but as it took speed, we heard again the call of the freight train, and then saw its yellow spotlight moving swiftly along in the dark.

"No!" whispered Marietta, in stricken knowledge.

The two machines moved in perfect convergence. The engineer must have seen the car lights charging toward the crossing, for he began to sound his whistle again, at first in long wails, and then, as the distance closed with steady swiftness, in short hoots. He sent the engine bell rolling. His brakes began to shriek.

"Max!" cried Marietta and began to run away from the living design of the right angle which was about to meet itself at the crossing of the quarry road and the tracks of the Olympia spur line. But just as quickly she turned and ran back to me, and was with me when the lights of the car flew into the air before they went out, and when after a long minute we heard the metallic impact which was muffled by the meadow. There was then silence except for the rolling of the locomotive bell which continued to terrorize the night even after the heavy train screamed itself to a standstill.

※ ※ ※

So, late that night, all the details of excitement, publicity, and grief over Max which I had lived through the night before now came true.

After the crash I ran to Mr Standish's door to ask for a car to go to the crossing. He was home and drove us. In the distance we saw lights come on in the Dana house. At the crossing the train was halted blocking the road. We saw lanterns swinging from the hands of the trainmen, and all too soon as we approached we saw the wreckage and heard the outraged plaints of the train crew—"ran right in front of us and stopped."

"Perhaps the car engine stalled?"

"—Can't say as to that. Stopped smack on the tracks is all."

Nothing could be moved until Doctor Osborne and county police arrived. The concertina was caught in a bush.

"Where is he?" I asked the engineer.

"Over there by the bushes."

"Is he . . . ?"

"Oh, yes. Instantly."

Marietta wanted to see him. The engineer said,

"Oh, no, young lady. You don't want to."

I drew her away. Mr Standish walked on to the Dana house and made the necessary telephone calls. Doctor Osborne arrived in fifteen minutes. He sent me home in his car with Marietta and told me to wait for him there. We sat in his car in front of his house saying nothing until he arrived, driven by Mr Standish, almost an hour later. He took Marietta upstairs and I waited for him. Presently he returned and drove me to Newstead. There it would be his sad honor to tell Alicia the news before the press, alerted by the police, began to ring up for colorful background. He would not tell Uncle Alec, who had retired early under heavy sedation. We later heard how Doctor Osborne knocked at the bedroom door and entered. There was a night light burning. Softly he said, "Alicia, dear?" Instantly she replied, "It's Max!"

"How is Marietta?" I now asked him.

"She is asleep. I had to give her something. She is very

highly keyed nervously, as you may have seen. —Would you describe what happened?"

I tried to speak flatly but my own excitement made me incoherent and he had to ask questions. In the course of these it came out that Max had acted oddly at the quarry the night before.

"You mean," said Doctor Osborne, "that you speculated about his committing suicide?"

"Not in so many words, but, yes, I did think of it."

"Had he seemed depressed?"

"Well, at times, and then again, sort of wild."

"M'm." He was a tall, heavy man with a square, ruddy face in which his eyes were large, patient, and kind. His voice had the burry resonance which many medical men and priests seem to develop from years of professional enunciation of arcane formulas. "Wild: how?"

I told him about Max's playing tag with the train on my first afternoon at Newstead. He listened with searching speculation in his eyes. Then,

"I see. You gather it was not the first time he had played such a game with the engineer?"

"No, it was not the first time."

"I see. So perhaps he was doing the same thing tonight, if he was in the same 'wild' mood?"

"I suppose yes, it is possible."

"Yes, it would be quite like him. —Do you think you could make this as an assertion which would result in a statement of accidental death?"

"Why, I suppose so."

"It is a distinct possibility; and we have no firm information on which to base an assumption of suicide."

"No, sir."

"Thank you. I was not there, but you were. It will be a comfort to Mrs Chittenden, if anything can be, to hear that it was an accident."

But as we looked at each other, we saw another answer; and by this conspiracy I was mercifully distracted for a little while from my own feeling of sickness and horror at my cousin's death.

Newstead was dark except for the fingers of light thrown by the bronze lantern high in the towering main porch. As we entered the silent house where troubled sleep must now yield to waking into nightmare, Doctor Osborne asked,

"Are you all right now?"

"Yes."

"Try to get some sleep. We're all going to need you tomorrow. Try to see Marietta. This is very rough on her."

"Yes, sir."

"Good night, old man."

Nobody had ever called me that, and I had never heard it outside the theater or novels. It was just the trifle to brace me so that I could feel like a true man doing his part—for the first time—to preserve the order, justice, and mercy of the world in a time of trouble.

But as I was quieting to sleep, with an odd ringing in my ears which would not go away when I turned my head from side to side on my pillow, I became aware, with puzzled shame, that my emotion was avowing itself in a new turn. Every secret fold of the hills in the late and again silent night spoke to me of the places of desire; and with the patience of lust I invited visions and schemes; and because these had more to do with life than death, I felt false to the sorrow of that house, and could not desist but dreamed on awake, wondering if she was also sleepless, whether in Max's name, or—so clear was my fantasy—mine.

❧ ❧ ❧

By unspoken agreement neither Marietta nor I ever told anybody about Max and the dead dog.

❧ ❧ ❧

Late the next morning came a note, typed by Miss Magruder and initialed by Aunt Lissy.

Richard my dear,

forgive me if I do not see you for the present. I am sure you understand. I know what you must feel for all of us, and for yourself. Say a prayer for me and ask my dear Rose if she will do so too. I am sure you are now eager to go home, but I would be grateful if you would remain until after the services tomorrow, and it would help me very much if you would be with me then. There will be no one else but the family, including, of course, the Osbornes. My poor boy, how sorry we all are to have brought you here only to know tragedy. You must put it all out of your thoughts when you are home again. Devotedly,

A.C.

I went to the Osbornes' for dinner that evening. Marietta
looked like a ghost. Whenever I caught her eyes she silently
implored me to forgive her—for what, I did not know. Her
mother, a weathered, gristly woman whose chief interest
was breeding jumpers and showing them, was nervous at
the hovering solemnity of the time, and in her inability to let
us alone, she conducted a running monologue about prepa-
rations for the horse show to be held in early September. She
wanted Marietta to ride Cavalier Girl.

"She jumps so beautifully," said Mrs Osborne, and we did
not know whether she referred to horse or rider. "Wouldn't
you come back for it?" she asked me.

"No, he wouldn't," said Marietta.

"But we'd love to have him."

"No. We must never expect him here again."

Doctor Osborne intervened.

"There was a cable from Lina this afternoon," he said.

"Oh? Did they notify her?"

"Alicia cabled her."

"Is she coming?"

"No—not now. If they need her later—"

"I see. So sensible. —How is Alexander?"

"It is sad to see him."

"I don't suppose he will be able to go tomorrow?"

"No, I have advised against it."

"It's really better, isn't it. He might really collapse, as he
does."

"I am not going," said Marietta.

"Mar, my dear: you cannot mean it."

"I do."

"But Max—your own—"

"I know. But I hate funerals. And I would be false to him if I went. I know how he felt about such things, too."

"But for Alicia's sake."

"I know. I'm sorry. But she will understand."

"Then she is more clever than I. I simply don't understand how you—"

"We'll see," said Doctor Osborne mildly.

Mrs Osborne took a deep breath to proclaim her essential health in the presence of so much odd feeling. Her bony breast rose wholesomely, and on the oakleaf brown of her skin her strand of pearls showed white as good teeth.

☙ ☙ ☙

After dinner,

"Richard and I are going for a little ride in my car," said Marietta.

There were no objections, for which I was glad, because she seemed in a state of utmost urgency, and another wrangle would have been hard to endure.

She asked me to drive, saying,

"I'll tell you where to go. There's a back road by the river. I want to feel *away!*"

She sat for a few minutes with her hands over her face. She seemed to be making a brave effort to recover herself. Finally she said,

"Nobody ever told me how exhausting grief is," she said. "And yet I can't be still for a minute. I can't. —I will die of home unless I can leave it when I must, and come back when I can!"

I remember the hot density of the night, and the fireflies more wonderfully profuse than ever, and how we took a road I had not been on, and came out beyond the meadow to a small river blacker than the meadow where mist and fireflies hovered. "Turn here," she said, and we went along under overhanging trees, following the river for miles toward the city of Calverton, Delaware. "Now that way," and we could begin to see a glow above the city, and I remembered how the streets had looked on the day Max met my train there. "There, turn off here," and we entered an aisle of deep shadow in the darkest groves between the country and the city. Now we could see outskirts across open fields and towers of lights, and then suddenly, a great shuddering flare of firelight which revealed the stacks and domes, the lofts and ranked retorts of a steel mill. They were pouring molten metal from the Bessemer converters, and though we remained in the night-shaded trees, the whole sky beyond us was like a curtain lighted by flames. As we looked the sky went dark again except for an updraft of sparks which went out in their turn. Our lane narrowed, and then we had to stop. The river was beyond the grove. Some obstacle to the current made a ruffle of water and sound.

"Now we are *away*," I said.

"Oh, yes. Richie—"

"What:"

"He called you Richie from the beginning."

"Yes."

"So did I."

Her voice sounded as if it were choked with unsought tenderness—a sign of tyrannical desire, a matter of wonder in that time of grief, and yet impossible to deny. Our hearts began to beat together. In that sooty thicket, by the tarnished river, under the vast sky waverings of the distant furnaces, we escaped into each other from that summer. Much of the world's literature has been expended in search of metaphor which will recall and hold forever the instant of love's consummation. At first, then, I became the cereus, laboring to leave the long sleep of neutral preparation, and almost with suffering to approach the release of petals which would seem to give their own white light. And then I became the fountain of light itself, like one of the innocent rockets over Newstead; and when I fell through darkness in the exquisite extinction of her embrace, with her I entered into the kingdom of earth.

꙰ ꙰ ꙰

How was it then possible to leave our transfigured waste-land and return to Chittenden Hills?

But we must and we did, though we paused several times to be silent together, or to talk in assuaged small words which spoke of nothing great, and asked little. Max was never far from our thoughts.

"Richie," she said, "is it possible? Will we die, too?"

She did not think of when or how, only of the large question. That she asked it seemed to me another way of affirming what we had affirmed against death, in love's way.

I replied, "We will, but how lucky that we don't know when."

"He knew, but he couldn't help it," she said.

"I know."

"When did you first have any thought about it?" she asked.

"Death?"

"Yes."

I saw again, then, a vision out of my extreme childhood, and told her of it. When we had to go downtown in Dorchester long ago, we would go to the corner of our street and take the Elmwood Avenue streetcar. We often had to wait and I would gaze along the tracks in the direction from which the car would come. I first understood what was meant by "distance" as I followed the lines of the tracks converging at infinity, and when in school we had drawing exercises in perspective, I always saw the streetcar tracks instead of the plain black lines which started here, far apart, and receded, there, to the vanishing point. It was marvelous to think about a vanishing point, and how all things went away to it. But even more marvelous was the notion which struck me one day watching for the streetcar—the notion that *things might come from the vanishing point toward me*. What was it like, there, where things vanished, and where did they wait until it was time for them to follow the black lines—the car tracks—which would bring them to me? I never took my eyes off the blurred point far down the straight vista of Elmwood Avenue where the car tracks converged, for if I looked hard enough perhaps I might see some great hand setting the streetcar suddenly on the tracks and starting it off. But I never caught this happening, and it was always a surprise which I felt viscerally when I saw the object moving toward me out of the mote-trembling distance. One day watching it in its delayed approach, I saw what it looked like—it was like a yellow skull, and the idea that a skull was moving along the streetcar tracks did not seem at all strange. It was wide and bulging at the top, and it had two absolutely empty eye places, and an empty nose place, and under that, it narrowed to a jaw without a mouth but with a kindly smile showing long pieces like teeth. Under it was shadow along which it glided and rocked, with, of course, the many stops for people at street corners far up the line. It was a patient skull, not frightening, for it preserved its smile, like the one on pirate flags or poison labels. It kept this image until always at about the same place each time it assumed the familiar likeness of the streetcar seen from the front. The wires overhead began humming, we could hear the bell tone of the metal wheels on the rails, and when it stopped at the corner of Herkimer Avenue and then started again toward us, magically I saw only the yellow front of the streetcar, with its two cavernous windows, its dark headlight, and its almost perpendicular cowcatcher. But I knew what a skull was, and that it was something about death, which had nothing to do with me.

"Let's never believe it ever will have," said Marietta.

※ ※ ※

The memorial services for my cousin were brief and private. In a transept of the Episcopalian Cathedral of St John the Divine in the city, I stood with Aunt Lissy and heard with bowed head the ritual of mortal consignment, read out of the Book of Common Prayer. Her strength and calm were remarkable. She seemed ageless and insubstantial.

If a bitter peacefulness now possessed her, perhaps it was because she was able to grieve for the dead instead of for the living.

When it was time to go, she walked leaning on my arm. Her pace was infinitely slow, and I felt strain in my muscles from working to keep step with her. At the door she thanked the Dean who had conducted the service, spoke briefly and gratefully to the Doctor and Mrs Osborne, and tenderly asked them to tell Marietta that she understood her absence. Then she let me help her into her car.

"Richard? Could you accompany me?" she asked in a voice whispery with fatigue.

I entered the car and sat beside her. Frazier closed the limousine door and we drove off toward Newstead. My cousin held her gaze away from me, seeing or not seeing the gray streets pass by until we reached the country. A black veil so thin that it looked like the color of smoke covered her head and shoulders, and seemed to remove her far away. I felt I must not look at her if she so clearly wanted to keep silence and privacy; yet I could not help watching her and I felt desperately that I should think of the suitable things to say at a time like that. Luckily nothing occurred to me, however hard I tried. When at last we left the post road for the country lanes leading homeward, Aunt Lissy forced herself to take strength out of nowhere by drawing two or three deep breaths, and then said,

"Richard, how strange and wonderful to have you here just now—somehow you have become the whole family. Will you help me with one more difficult matter?"

"Yes—" My word must have sounded as my eyes felt—open and awed by mystery.

"Thank you, my dear. Let me tell you."

Maximilian's body had been cremated before the memorial service in the Cathedral. His ashes were present in a small bronze urn inside a cubic box of polished ebony which rested on the front seat of the limousine next to Frazier. She could not bear the idea of a burial service, and certainly it was intolerable to think of preserving the ashes morbidly in their urn. She had no illusions about the immortality of any material thing—her faith in the spirit was enough to bring her peace in time. But now in her sorrow she searched for some gesture of freedom for Maximilian's mortal residue. If there was no way to work some act of justice to sanction the tragic waste of so young a life with its form so comely, she obeyed the old blind impulse of seeking to do for the dead what the living might have wanted. Could I help her by thinking of what to do with her son's ashes? It was extraordinary, they all decided, how well I seemed to know him in so little time.

I was made obscurely uneasy by what she said and what she sought, but it was the subject of death, really, which I shrank from. Death to me at that age was an obscenity. I did not know the reasonableness it carried with it into the thoughts of those who were within hailing distance of it. My manners helped me at the moment to recall that persons in grief often behaved oddly, and with almost hearty politeness, I said,

"I'll try to help, Aunt Lissy."

She touched my hand, expecting a further answer then and there. Behind her veil her eyes were deeply far away but their determined light shone with the extremity of her fatigue and her desire to consummate her son's life and death. I searched my thought. I saw Max in his utmost self. I said,

"Aunt Lissy? I think I know what I would do."
"Yes: yes: tell me."

❧ ❧ ❧

So it was that late that morning after Aunt Lissy had
retired to her apartment at Newstead, I was driven by
Frazier to the top of the ridge which gave the first view of
the quarry. There I left the car, carrying the ebony casket.
As I started down the ragged trail toward the lake, Frazier
said,

"Do you mind if I come along, Mr Richard?"

"No. Not at all."

He followed me. Of all those at Newstead, he had seemed
to be Max's closest friend. Hitherto I had seen only the back
of his head and neck and shoulders in Aunt Lissy's car. He
was a well-built young Englishman with shiny black hair,
strong facebones, a ball chin, and pink, scrubbed skin. Now
he carried in hand his chauffeur's cap—a gesture of respect,
for we were about to commit mortal remains, and his sense
of the occasion sought to make ceremony for it. In silence
we came to the Peninsula, and I walked out to the tip.

The lake was like dark glass under the misty noonday
heat. I looked down and could see nothing of the depths.
The stillness was pure and entranced. I handed the ebony
box to Frazier. When he had hold of it, I opened the box and
took out a small but heavy bronze urn which had a lid like a
cone. The whole vessel was elaborately ornamented with
Christian symbols. I looked for hinges but there were none,
and I found that the lid came off by twisting. The bronze

fitting turned in its grooves with velvety smoothness. Open, the urn revealed its contents—a modest double handful of gray ash with specks of hard matter which must have been fragments of bone.

I kneeled down at the water's edge and with lid in one hand and urn in the other I let both down into the water slowly and gently. When the water entered about the ashes, I let go of the bronze pieces. They sank, creating with astonishing swiftness a small eddy which swirled upward. Most of the ashes were caught in the spiral current before they sank, and showed as gray cloud, roiling in the shape of those forms so often drawn for drapery or folds of garment by William Blake. A thin residue of ash—the lightest particles —floated on the surface and created a silvery drift which held the light of day like the humid air itself. If I had thought the lake to rest in perfect stillness, I now saw by the drift of the weightless ash that it was never still, for the invisible currents which turned so slowly along the limestone shore now took the thin film of ash aside and away and out toward the center of the quarry lake where it was soon lost in the small distance.

I was oddly without thought or feeling at the moment of performing my task for my cousin. The quarry seemed eternal and all things there—dust in the rocky walls, dwarf trees growing from crevices, the cold lake water coming from springs far below and evaporating into the air which became sky far above, the silence, the last presence of my Cousin Max—seemed to enter the present tense forever.

"—For Thine is the kingdom, and the power, and the glory, forever. Amen," I heard behind me. Frazier finished his prayer audibly. I turned to look at him, admiring his unself-conscious propriety. He returned my look sturdily.

His blue eyes were intense and dark with emotion under control.

"That's raght," he said, in his Londoner's accent. "It's where he ought to be."

I nodded and we returned to the car. Frazier held open the door for me to enter the limousine cabin where I had ridden from Newstead. But I shook my head and said,

"May I ride up front with you?"

He seemed pleased, and as we returned to the house, he sought relief in chattering to me. He and Max were great friends, they were. He had come from England when Max was twelve years old with a consignment of British motorcars for Newstead and had remained ever after, first as mechanic, later as chauffeur, and best of all, as a sort of hired chum for Max. He laughed. Max it was who did most of the chumming, in the sense of teaching things not hitherto known. For just one example, Max at fifteen had taught him how to play blackjack, and had won most of his wages from him week after week, but that had to stop when the time came for Frazier and his girl—one of the upstairs maids at the house—to get married. He and the boy remained good pals, and everything had looked so bright for the coming year at Harvard, for Max had leased a house in Cambridge, and had planned to take Frazier, as houseman, and his wife, as cook, and Patrick O'Boin, the valet, back with him when the college year began again, and they had all looked forward to a lordly time of it. Now Frazier didn't know: he had not said anything to the Madam yet, it was too soon, but he had had his American citizenship for three years now, and he had talked it over with Mrs F., and he had got some idea of what this country was all about, and he rather thought he would give notice in the autumn, and go into politics—starting modestly, of course, with some job in the municipal government of Calverton, or perhaps Philadelphia. He looked at me obliquely to wonder what I thought of all this talk, and of such an ambitious prospect.

"When everything changes," he said in extenuation, "it's best, I always say, to make a clean break of it. You know, sir?"

In his way, he measured Max's absence.

I nodded seriously.

※ ※ ※

In early afternoon they said Uncle Alec wanted to see me before I left.

He was lying in an armchair in his sitting room at the opposite end of the house from my quarters. Though the day was heavy with thundery heat, he wore a dressing gown with a fur collar, and a wood fire was burning in the grate at his feet. By his side was a low round table piled with books in magnificent bindings. A huge dislike reading glass lay on opened pages. He was as pale as bone china, with a glossy luster over his skin which suggested extreme age, though as I had last seen him he merely seemed a man well past middle age, frail but durable. He was certainly thinner than he had been two nights ago. Neurotics can impersonate health as well as illness, but they must always have a stimulating pretext. I could not imagine what would ever occur to unite Uncle Alec with vital concerns again. When he spoke to me it was with a thread of voice. At first, I had regarded him as grotesque; then as a memory of a man quite lost in time; now I saw him as a human being in extreme suffering, and I think I learned just then that I must never again content myself with an easy judgment, based on superficial evidence, of anyone else.

"Sit down, Richard, just for a moment. Such an end to our hopes. We hoped so much of you with our son. I thought it cruel when he fled our pahty, it quite sickened me. But now it is clee-ah that he was suffering from something which drove him to reckless acts until the accident which destroyed him."

He looked at me with his dimmed and dry eyes as if to discern any disagreement I might have about the terms of Max's death. I did not try to conceal anything—but my appalled and serious demeanor as I looked upon Uncle Alec in his wreckage made me seem to agree with him. Max's death must have been like the fall of a temple—the edifice of the family gods which in crashing to the ground and abolishing a future was most cruel when it failed to kill the last progenitor, the father himself.

"Yes. How difficult any farewells can be. Still, we must do our best to let you go with some kind recollection of Newstead. I believe you were fond of Maximilian. We know he instantly became devoted to you. So this."

He took up from his book table a little buckskin sac and handed it to me. With a palsied forefinger he indicated that I was to open it. I did so, and found a heavy polished gold ring which held a large dark red carnelian bearing in deep intaglio an heraldic design.

"That was Max's ring," he said. "He rarely wore it. I gave it to him on his twenty-first birthday. The seal is my family's device. Will you have it, my boy?" I hesitated out of amazement, not reluctance. He was short of energy and so spent more than he should have in impatience. "After all, we are cousins, you have a right to wear it, especially if I say so!"

Then I saw that he was in a remote way bestowing the ring on me as upon an heir, and I bowed and thanked him.

"Yes," he said. "That will do. —And this," he said, picking up an octavo book bound in blue leather with gold tooling. He riffled the pages weakly. "This was his, too. I could not bear to read more than a line or two, but my son wrote the notes and perhaps you would have it?"

He handed it to me and I glanced at the first page. A title was inscribed there. It read, "Detached Thoughts. By Charles James Maximilian Chittenden." It was a thick blank book, of fine rag paper. Only a few pages seemed to be written upon.

I thanked Uncle Alec.

"Let us have your news now and then," he said. "We shall always be interested in your progress. Do come back any time. How splendid if you should become a scholar, and have need of our books." A hot far glow appeared in his eyes, some fire of an ambition not yet taken from him, as so much had been taken. "That will endure, at least," he said with a brave effort at strong statement. "The Alexander and Alicia Chittenden Library will survive, even if none of us and nothing else ever will!"

"Yes. Thank you, Uncle Alec."

"May I see you wear the ring?"

"Oh, yes."

I put it on two fingers before I found one where it would fit, and then showed it to him. He took my hand and touched the ring.

"Thank you, dear Richard. Now you must go, or you will

be late. Everything is always too late. Come." He drew me toward him and to my embarrassed astonishment I felt his dry, scratchy lips on my cheek. It was like being kissed by straw. The tears started up in my eyes at the signs of love in one who had no one left to love.

"Good-by, Uncle Alec," I said, thickly.

"Good," he said, "you can feel. Never be ashamed to show feeling. Good-by, do go now, yes."

A mindless smile suddenly stretched his bony face, and he put up a finger to detain me after all. He worked his grapeish lips for a moment and then began to speak weakly, but with all the old social air of his delightful duty as master and expositor of the great library downstairs, where it had always been his pleasure to bring forth his best anecdotes for impressed visitors.

"One day the most peefectly killing thing happened," he said. "We had just engaged a new housekeeper, and Miss Magruder was showing her around the place. They came in here, and the housekeeper—she was a bony old thing got up in black alpaca—ran her finger along the table there looking for dust, and suddenly she saw the Leda there in the center." Uncle Alec pointed to where he saw the statue, and began to weep. "She saw the Sansovino of Leda and the Swan, and said to Miss Magruder"— Uncle Alec could hardly shape his words through the sobs which shook him like gasping coughs, and lost a few words from what he tried to say— "she said, '. . . *stars! . . . duck up to!*'"

He buried his face in his hands and rocked himself back and forth while his heartbroken sobs coughed through his fingers. The opposite ends of his world had suddenly met in his mind, short-circuited by grief. As he could not see me, I decided in panic that he was also invisible, and before he should reappear, I tiptoed out and ran down the corridor. I knew I would never see him again.

❦ ❦ ❦

Marietta was waiting to take me to my train.

Before we reached town I asked her to drive aside into a country lane.

"There's no use," she said, "Richie. Don't. It can't, no matter what we want."

She knew what I was hoping for. She continued on the high road.

"But it meant so much more," I protested.

"It always does, if one feels anything at all. And we did."

"Then why not?"

"No. The world would say no, and they would be right, and all we could do would be to protest, and I am tired of protesting."

"You are not that weak."

"Oh, but I am. And another thing."

She drove in silence, and I had to ask,

"What else is in our way?"

"You do surely know, dear Richie."

"No, I don't."

I reached for her and she gave me her cheek, but she kept driving.

"Then if I must: it is Max: we made love for him as much as for each other last night. You will realize that later if you don't now."

I was shocked, and exclaimed bitterly.

"No, you don't see," she insisted. "But when you think of everything that made us feel the way we did, you will see that it was not just you and me, but the whole thing, and he was at the center of it. —Don't you feel how exhausted I still am? That may really be what lifelong sorrow is."

She was not asking for pity or sympathy, but it was what I felt for her, even as I fed my sense of betrayal after what I had taken the night before as an avowal for a life. She had the knack of answering me when I said nothing.

"No, you see, you are a boy in his last year at school, and I am, in effect, a widow. Max said you understood how it had been with us ever since we were old enough. You cannot be surprised."

But I was surprised at last, and cruelly hurt. She felt this. She took my hand and kissed the inside of my wrist; her lips made her butterfly touch on my pulse.

"I am trained for life by him. You and I would never see anything the same way," she said. "You always see things standing in light and shadow, just things themselves. But he lived by opposites. Joy made him think of misery. Love of hate. All the rest. And now, it is the same with me. It would infuriate you. But there it is, and there I am. —When I am an old woman with a skin full of bones and a hectic laugh, I'll still be thinking of him, and I'll be married to a ghost."

It wasn't too long after that summer until I saw that she spoke the truth, for the ghost to whom she was married called out again and again. She looked for its likeness in life; married its approximation three times. Her husbands were all playboys, two of them foreign, all sleekly handsome, bland in their excesses, and just enough like the perturbèd spirit within her memory to mock her true quality. Forty years later she fulfilled her description of herself, though her eyes were still hungrily lovely, and the skull had never changed its fine bone.

But when we said good-by at the station I was still too close to the events and discoveries of my time there to yield them up easily; and I kissed her as if to change her mind. But she was stronger than I. We heard my train rumbling in on the platform above the street.

"Darling!" she cried, like someone wholesomely sending a boy off to school for all to hear. "Hurry, you'll miss it!"

If she had sent me away happy, I would never have noticed the manner of my going; but as it was, scrambling up the sticky iron stairs, I was painfully aware of my awkwardness, and when the porter handed me into the train, I was blushing so hotly that he shook his head at me, exhaled a comical sigh, and said richly, "It sho' do!" I wondered all the way to Philadelphia what he could have meant by that.

❀ ❀ ❀

Gradually the sound and movement of the train took away my immediate feeling. Soon I was looking for something to do, and I remembered the bound notebook which Uncle Alec had given me. I took it from my suitcase and began to read it.

The title page was lettered rather grandly in imitation of a published book:

DETACHED THOUGHTS
by
Charles James Maximilian Chittenden

and each page held a single brief entry written in his handwriting, which had a brisk, thorny look, in black ink. The entries ran for ten pages, as follows:

. . . *I like him, because, like myself, he seems a friendless animal.*

. . . *My whole life has been at variance with propriety, not to say decency; my circumstances are become involved; my friends are dead or estranged, and my existence a dreary void.*

[This] is written in an evening and morning in haste, with ill-health and worse nerves. I am so bilious, that I nearly lose my head, and so nervous that I cry for nothing; at least today I burst into tears, all alone by myself, over a cistern of goldfishes, which are not pathetic animals . . . I have been excited and agitated, and exhausted mentally and bodily all this summer, till I sometimes begin to think not only "that I shall die at the top first" [as Swift remarked of himself when he saw an elm withered in the upper branches] but that the moment is not very remote. I have no particular cause of griefs, except the usual accompaniments of all unlawful passions.

. . . *[She has] been dangerously ill; but it may console you to learn that she is dangerously well again.*

. . . *I am not sure that long life is desirable for one of my temper and constitutional depression of spirits, which of*

*course I suppress in society; but which breaks out when
alone, and in my writings, in spite of myself. It has been
deepened, perhaps, by some long past events.*

*. . . I am like the Tiger: if I miss the first spring, I go
growling back to my jungle again; but if I do hit, it is
crushing.*

*. . . I am violent but not malignant; for only fresh provo-
cations can awaken my resentments.*

*. . . A man and a woman make far better friendships
than can exist between two of the same sex; but these
with this condition, that they never have made, or are to
make, love with each other. Lovers may, and, indeed,
generally are enemies, but they can never be friends;
because there must always be a spice of jealousy and a
something of self in all their speculations. I indeed, I
rather look upon love altogether as a sort of hostile trans-
action. . . .*

*[What I write] may be now and then voluptuous: I can't
help that.*

There he was, in fragments, in those pages. I thought his
accent unmistakable, and he filled my thoughts to the
fullest, until for the first time I felt a real sorrow for him,

that thickened my throat and made me pretend to lean with excited interest close to the train window looking out to hide my feeling from any passenger who might be staring at me. Where before I had known horror at his death I now felt loss. How real a lost life could remain—perhaps we never lose anybody.

But it was not for a long time that I understood fully the purpose and meaning of those notebook jottings. One day in a later year I was reading the letters of Byron, and in a letter to his mother from Falmouth in June 1807, I came upon the phrase "a friendless animal," and I remembered Max's first entry. I compared the words—there, sure enough, was the exact statement with which Max began his little series of sketches in self-portraiture. With some excitement I hunted through the poet's letters and found every one of Max's entries—they were all quotations from letters to friends: Dallas, Hobhouse, Moore; to his publisher Murray; to his wife and an unnamed lady, written variously from Newstead Abbey, Bologna, Ravenna, Pisa, Albaro, ranging in date from 1807 to 1822. Moreover, I discovered that in an early Murray edition of Byron's collected works there was a section entitled "Detached Thoughts," which were autobiographical notes written in his last days at Ravenna. The manuscript of this was given by Byron to Lord Clare, his closest companion at Harrow, who came to pay him a visit at Montenero in 1822. Clare was commissioned to carry the manuscript to Murray in London. The two schoolmates never met again. "I have a presentiment that I shall never see him more," said Byron to Teresa Guiccioli, who saw that his eyes filled with tears at the thought. My cousin, steeped in the Byronic tradition and lore of the house, had found his counterpart. I found it piercingly sad that Max had turned to someone long dead to find emotions and actions which might help to account for his own. What a prison of loneliness he must have been in. Had he been idly drawn to Byron's style only to see it come all too true in himself?

How longingly they had all tried to explain my cousin's life—and death. With theories ranging in source from common sense and intuitive love, to restless systems in Viennese psychology, they brought their poor wisdom to the task, and found it insufficient. It seemed in the end most reasonable to conclude that romantic dislocation, whatever the cause, was a disease which existed, and could be recognized. It was even possible, as we have seen, to die of it, even if no one could remember or speak of what may have started it on its hidden life. The final impression I kept of him in after years was of a spirit struggling to appear, and whether it was a good spirit or an evil, I did not know, and the older I became, the less I wanted to make the distinction, for as I left my youth, I was no longer omniscient.

I was helped to that conclusion by another odd small circumstance. It was not until years later as I was leafing through Max's notebook to identify the passages in Byron that I found further entries in the last six pages. Separated from the Byron passages by a hundred blank pages, they had never come to sight before. These last entries were in blue ink and were more hastily inscribed. Except for the final one, they were to be found nowhere in Bryon, for I searched; but in any case, whenever written, what they all said belonged only to that summer:

. . . I saw a small, four-year-old boy, on crutches, strug-gling forward, bringing each crutch ahead in the awk-ward thrust of an upright insect. Two older and healthy

children were behind him. Suddenly he falls forward—nothing to sustain him. He falls direct to the earth—meets it with his cheek. The others bend to save or help him. Too late. I become that child, for a moment.

Why do I frighten him? Perhaps because of the different degrees of our apprehension of emotion.

We all see Byron in ourselves, even my father, however implausibly.

Only in autumn do I feel immemorial, when the year is dying. Never in spring, which seems prodigal, wasteful, of seed.

Autumn: when I see the death of the year transpire in such glory, why do I hesitate? Must I await my own autumn?

At the quarry:
>   *Though the night was made for loving,*
>   *And the day returns too soon,*
>   *Yet we'll go on more a-roving*
>   *By the light of the moon.*

※ ※ ※

At home for the rest of the summer, I felt that I was looked at with troubled but loyal recognitions. My parents had to hear every detail of what I could tell. They exclaimed repeatedly over Max's tragedy, and loved me the better because I lived. As I described what the newspapers had reported, they said, "Yes," already well-informed but eager to find *me* in all the events I told them of. It was like my mother to come rather dreamily to a loving acceptance of my new relation to Alicia and her family. My father exclaimed with impatient realism when she said,

"How nice if you could go back again. They really must have become quite fond of you. I imagine you can go back all your life, at any time."

But even if I had wanted to, any return in the long future was made impossible by further changes which no one had foreseen. The family's posterity was lost as the years broke over its memories. Who is ever prepared for change? If it is to be met without surprise, it must first be imagined. No one thought of what would at last become of Newstead. In our cousinship we came to know all the details of how Uncle Alec's and Aunt Lissy's posterity was denied to them —and to me, should I ever have wanted to return to Chittenden Hills.

Aunt Lissy died in 1927, and Uncle Alec in 1931. Lina di Gregorio was the sole heir. There was nothing to bring her back to Chittenden Hills, and everything to keep her away. She had no need to sell the place to bring her a fortune, for the rest of her inheritance made her richer than even her husband could ask. She found a satisfactory outcome to her real estate problem when she encountered in

Rome the agent of what many believed to be a providential solution.

It came about through the busy goodness of a friend of her mother's and mine. This lady, a devout and imaginative widow, with an eye to her personal salvation, decided to live out her days in Rome. Her name was Mrs Cornelia O'Shea. In the course of years she had made for herself a formidable position whose obscurity was its strength. She lived on the delights of burrowing helpfully in the tunnels of Roman ecclesiastical politics. When she was awarded the Cross of Honor "Pro Ecclesia et Pontifice" she sent a copy of her papal citation to my mother with exclamation marks dashed along the margin. "Nell O'Shea!" exclaimed my mother. "Imagine!"

Princess Lina happened to meet her at an evening party in Rome and received her condolences on the death of the last member of her immediate family. Mrs O'Shea wondered what would become of her old friend's magnificent property, which she had never visited, but which she knew well through photographs in fashion magazines. As it happened, Nell O'Shea knew the Pro-Secretary to the Abbot General of the Calixtines in Rome. It appeared that the Order had plans to establish in America a priory or monastery whose continuing mission would be the renewal of the Christian ideal of matrimony as a sacrament.

A year later the work of Nell O'Shea was done, for Princess Lina deeded the property to the Order, and within two more years of remodelings and improvements, as they said, the members of the Priory were able to enter upon their mission in surroundings which I would have found difficult to reconcile with my memories of Newstead.

Sets of postcards were sold, with other souvenirs, at the Priory tourist shop, and a caption read: "Part monastery, part church, part experimental farm, and above all, part guesthouse of unexampled magnificence, the great estate of Newstead Priory sits imperially on its hill." Another told how the house had guest accommodations for thirty couples at a time. And more: carriage house and garages were converted into administrative offices, with a new blacktop parking area behind. "Literature" told that a feature of the main floor of the mansion was what was formerly the library. It had once contained the country's most distinguished collection of materials relating to the English poet Lord Byron. The collection was disposed of at public auction, realizing a handsome return for the Priory from purchases by leading university libraries and various private collectors at home and abroad. The library became the assembly hall of the Marriage Counseling Conference, where group retreats were held, and films were shown dramatizing marital problems which were used as a basis for seminar discussions. The vast dining room was converted into a cafeteria-style refectory, equipped with Monel Metal steam serving counters, an electric deep-fat fryer, and wood-grained Formica-top tables to accommodate sixty at a sitting. A chapel was installed at the rear of the mansion, with a sweeping view of the valley.

From that point the relaxing visitors could see in the distance the towering walls of the greenhouse, which still retained specimens from the famous collection of exotic plants brought together by the late owners. These included a small grove of banana palms, citrus trees—orange, lemon, and lime—and a rare plant of the cactus family (*cereus grandiflora*), and a few varieties of rare orchids.

I remember how the newspapers of the time were full of stories of a bitter family quarrel over the disposal of Newstead. Two of the other Chittenden brothers brought suit to void the gift made by Princess Lina, claiming that certain zoning laws must prevent the establishment of any institution in Chittenden Hills. Editorials raised the issue of religious prejudice. The wrangle was carried through the courts and my father referred to the affair as "an exercise in the higher squalor," causing my mother to exclaim in admiration, "Why, Dan!" In the end, as the daughter's wish prevailed, my Newstead vanished. Nell O'Shea could never have known what ironies were consequent upon her ardent efforts along the curial galleries.

❦ ❦ ❦

As that summer waned, I felt much older, but I thought it strange that this did not draw me closer in age to my father and mother. I saw them no longer as beautiful ageless parents with a happy boy, but as an older couple whose son felt like a man.

My mother shed tears now and then for Aunt Lissy, and, I think, for my lost childhood, and she murmured about how I must feel at the death of one near my own age.

My father showed a frowning solemnity at life's hardness, but his standards were not softened to accommodate suffering. When with thoughtless satisfaction I showed Uncle Alec's ring, my father said,

"It is a very handsome ring, a nice keepsake of the summer. But I'd rather have you wear *mine* someday."

He made a fist toward himself and looked at his heavy gold seal ring where his initials were engraved with flourishes. He took my gaze with him. We were both looking at the honor of a family and its succession—the honor which waits upon death at home.

He also looked at me now and then from under one cocked eyebrow—that expression which made him so handsomely attractive to the wives of his friends; and from that time on he ceased using my boyhood nickname, for something he read in my face and in my body's gesture, and a note he heard in my voice, told him that the time had come and gone, the moment which fathers wonder about, which he could never speak of, when his burgeoning son would have broken man's common secret of the flesh. The nearest he came to referring to the matter, in his mixed emotions of secret pride, humorous speculation, chagrin, and concern for my soul, was when he said, on the first Saturday after my return, "Richard, are you going to confession?"

꙰ ꙰ ꙰

As the first hint of autumn came off the lake on chill, misty morning winds, I began to feel zest for the season and the approach of my last year at school. I presently knew that I had been wounded, and that I was recovering; and I had moments of meditation in which, if I could have stated my thoughts clearly, I made up prayers which meant something like this: "Lord, keep me safe from powers I do not understand. Let me never destroy any living thing in the name of lost love."

But presently the fears behind these pleas went away, and I was able to remember Newstead in peace. Time mosses over even the most sorrowful events, until long afterward people speak of them in the most ordinary expressions of acceptance which do the work of moss in another way, joining experience and survival, rock and earth, together in gentled contours. If my father and mother spoke of Max, I would shake my head as they shook theirs, and in silence agree with their last word, and the world's, about my cousin; for without any reserved thought or remembered pang behind it, they all said that it was a pity he had to go, when he had everything to live for.

❈   ❈

❈

[215]